I0721867

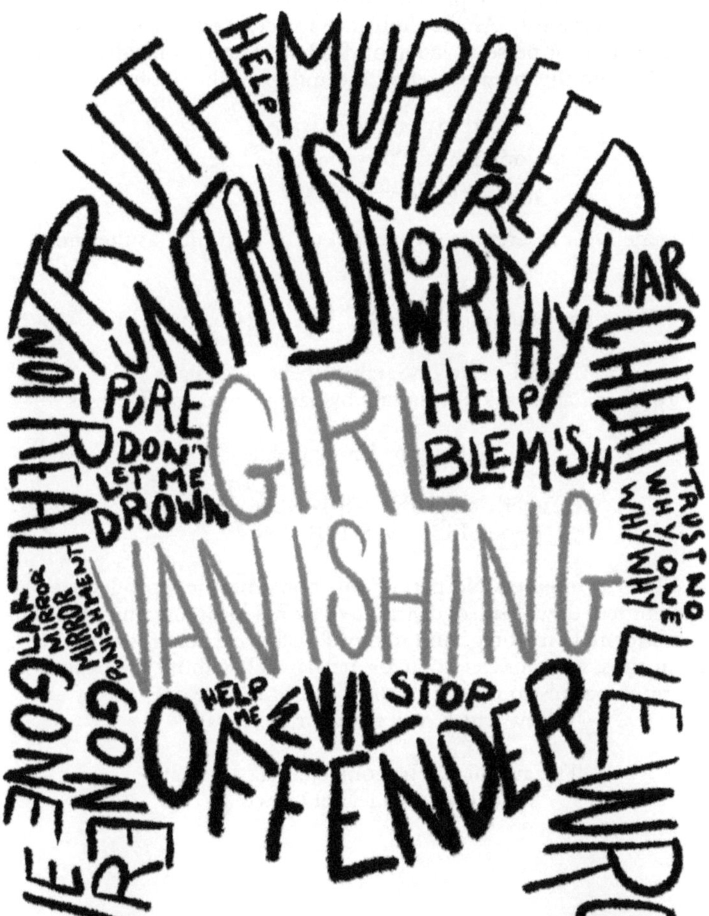

MADELINE DYER

This book is a work of fiction. Names, characters, places, and incidents either are the product of the author's imagination or are used fictitiously. Any resemblance to actual events, locales, organizations, or persons, living or dead, is entirely coincidental and beyond the intent of either the author or the publisher.

GIRL, VANISHING
Copyright © 2024 Madeline Dyer
All rights reserved.

Madeline Dyer asserts the moral right to be identified as the author of this work.

This First Edition published in June 2024 by Ineja Press.

Cover Design by Sarah Anderson Designs
Interior Paperback Formatting by Sarah Anderson Designs

Editing by Emily Colin

Paperback ISBN: 978-1-912369-50-8
eBook ISBN: 978-1-912369-49-2

All rights reserved. No part of this book may be reproduced, transmitted, downloaded, distributed, stored in or introduced into any information storage and retrieval systems, in any forms or by any means, whether electronic or mechanical, without the express written permission of the author, except for the purpose of a review which may quote brief passages.

The author can be contacted via email at
Madeline@MadelineDyer.co.uk

GIRL VANISHING

MADELINE DYER

INEJA PRESS

TITLES AVAILABLE FROM MADELINE DYER

The Untamed Series
Untamed
Fragmented
Divided
Destroyed
A Dangerous Game
This Vicious Way
The Threat of the Hunt

Roseheart Ballet Academy Series
The Rhythm of My Soul
Swans in the Dark

The Spirit of Fire Series
Spirit of Fire
Blood of the Phoenix

Standalone Books
The Curse of the Winged Wight
Inside the Night
Captive
Girl, Vanishing

Anthologies
Unbound
Being Ace

Writing as Elin Annalise
In My Dreams
My Heart to Find
It's Always Been You
Forever is Now

For the girls

people think they can hurt

TUESDAY, DECEMBER 3RD, 2013
WHEN THE BAD STUFF ENDS

Content Warnings

Mental illness, self-harm, suicidal ideation,
sexual abuse, and murder.

This is How it Ends

YOU'RE RUNNING. SWEAT IS POURING DOWN your back, Kira, drenching your shirt. Your arms pump frantically at your sides. You feel the first lingers of lactic acid burning into your thighs, and the lactic acid has a haughty face, and it's laughing and saying: You really thought it would be this easy? You really thought you could stop the murders?

I don't just *hear* the thoughts in your head; they wrap around me, strangle me. They become me.

But you did stop the murders—in a way. You stopped him, but you caused more.

Your fault, Kira.

You keep running. Your bare feet slap the pavement, and you're emitting a strange high-pitched noise as you run. You can feel the blood on your hands, and it's like a layer of PVA glue *sticking to you, and soon you'll be able to peel that layer off, just as you did in primary school, and then I can step out of this body and leave the darkness behind.*

It's all I want to do, to leave you.

But I can't.

We're in it for the long-haul, girl. You and me.

So, when you turn left, I turn left with you, and you think you can leave the Bad Stuff behind, but we both know that isn't true.

Imprisonment

THEY SAID IT WOULD BE QUICK.

But it isn't quick in reality, and it isn't quick in my dreams. My nightmares.

Because they press the scalding metal to my forehead, over and over again, as I cry and scream and beg. As my skin sizzles and crisps, as the smell of burning flesh curls inside my nostrils.

One letter isn't enough.

THE POSSIBLE RESULTS OF THE DETECTOR ROOM TESTING

PURE (P)

noun

An individual who scores perfectly during testing for the desirable qualities and will never be an Offender nor belong to the other Lower groups.

UNTRUSTWORTHY (U)

noun

A person who is programmed to prefer lies and deception to truth and honesty. Such programming can be detected from a young age via Testing before these traits take over. Early segregation of Untrustworthies can prevent these individuals from becoming Offenders. Untrustworthies make up a significant proportion of the Lower Population.

MANIPULATOR (M)

noun

A person who exhibits manipulative personality traits for their own selfish benefits. Testing can detect such traits. Testing can distinguish between Egocentrics and Manipulators, but sometimes an individual may be marked as both. Close monitoring of Manipulators can prevent these individuals from becoming Offenders.

EGOCENTRIC (E)

noun

A person who is self-centered with little regard for the feelings, desires, or needs of other individuals. Testing can distinguish between Egocentrics and Manipulators, but sometimes an individual may be marked as both. Close monitoring of Egocentrics can prevent these individuals from becoming Offenders.

CONCEITED (C)

noun

A person who is unduly full of their own self-importance, holding an excessive view of their own self-worth. Conceiteds are usually given the same rights as Pures, though this is not always the case in practice.

OFFENDER (O)

noun

An individual who has committed a crime. Usually this individual is an Untrustworthy, but occasionally Manipulators, Egocentrics, and very rarely Conceiteds will become Offenders, too. The 'O' will be added to the end of their existing brand (UO, MA, EO, or CO). Should a Pure individual commit a crime, the 'P' will be removed from their brand and they will simply be an 'O.' All Offenders will be sent straight to The De Hewitt Facility. Those who have committed minor crimes have the chance of being treated and healed at The De Hewitt Facility. Those with major crimes will be imprisoned for life.

HEALED OFFENDERS (H)

noun

An Offender who has been successfully treated and healed at the De Hewitt Facility. Only Offenders who committed minor crimes, such as theft or fraud, are eligible for the Healing Program at the De Hewitt Facility. Upon successful completion of this program, the individual's 'O' brand will be replaced with 'H' (UH, MH, EH, CH, or H). This individual will be released back into society, though they will be part of the Lower Population and restricted to The Lowers' housing.

THE LOWERS

collective noun

The Lower Population consists of all Untrustworthies, Offenders, and Healed Offenders. Some individuals from the following groups also belong to the Lowers: Manipulators, Egocentrics, and more rarely, Conceiteds. It should be noted that not all individuals belonging to the latter three sectors will live among Lowers in designated Lowers' housing; many will live with the Pures if their testing shows only low levels of programming for the undesirable qualities.

TUESDAY, JANUARY 14TH, 2014
FIVE WEEKS AFTER MISS
TAYLOR'S ADMISSION TO THE
DE HEWITT FACILITY

The Waspkeeper

"WRITING FEELS SAFER," I SAY. "WRITING WHAT I feel. What I think. Writing what I want to be. What I want to happen." My voice is slow, sluggish, and I stare at the notebook. Stare at the words I've already written: MIRROR MIRROR ON THE WALL, WHO IS THE FAIREST OF THEM ALL?

I don't know why I wrote those words. The silly fairy tale Mum would tell me.

See? I've messed up already. Writing something so stupid.

I'm messed up, and the mess will never go away.

Because I'm crazy. Everyone says it, thinks it.

No. You're not. It's the medication they've given you. That's all it is. You can't see the world for what it is. But you need to. You need to get out.

I sigh and look at Matt, the man on the other side of the desk, the man who's supposed to be helping me. But time isn't working quite right here—never does anymore. It's all distorted, stretched out.

Matt doesn't look like a Matt, with the dark hair sprouting from his chin and the even darker curly hair on top of his head and his huge horn-rimmed glasses. He looks like an Adrian. I don't like it when people look different to what they should be.

"And that's what you're doing now, Kira?" Matt asks, looking over those horn-rimmed glasses. His eyes are like wasps behind glass, and the wasps are watching me. But Matt never stings. He's the nicest one here.

He's got a pen in his hand also, but his is a fountain pen and I'm not allowed to use those. Not Worthy enough. And I know Matt's notebook doesn't contain stupid words like mine does. No, his contains the stuff on *me*. The observations and reports and his opinions, because he has to report back to the officials. But it's not fair that his opinions mean the difference between my freedom and prolonged entrapment.

I shrug when I realize he's waiting for an answer. "I think so. Though this is just silly." I shut my notebook and look up.

There's a corkboard behind Matt, and he's got all his celebrity selfies taped up there. Rihanna. Justin Timberlake. Barack Obama—though that one looks like Matt was posing with a cardboard cutout. Beyoncé. Leticia Dean. And some old man I don't recognize. But Matt's face is there, grinning away.

He's not grinning now though. He's waiting. Waiting for me to talk. Or write.

"Why is this silly?" he prompts, and I look at the lines around his mouth. They seem deeper today, somehow, like a tiny person has dug out trenches there. Maybe a waspkeeper has done it, wielding the shovel... I frown.

Waspkeeper.

I don't know where that came from. My hand itches to write the word.

"Kira?" Matt prompts, but I can't answer him until I've got my own answers. And what was I thinking about... Do wasps have keepers? Or is that just bees? I am not sure, but I need to know. I can't continue until I am sure...

Sure about what, Kira?

It's *her* voice, inside me. She sounds annoyed.

What am I thinking about?

The wasps. Yes. Waspkeeper. Or maybe a beekeeper, then. Yes. I shake my head to clear it. Like a beekeeper has got a little shovel and has been tunnelling out the grooves around Matt's mouth, trying to make deeper channels so water can collect.

Why water?

I don't know. Everything is always so confusing now.

Matt must be thirsty. That's why the waspkeeper or beekeeper or whatever it is wants to collect water, *is* collecting water.

I'm thirsty. My mouth is dry. Everyone's thirsty here all the time. Thirsty for life and freedom and just to be treated kindly.

FOCUS

"KIRA, I NEED YOU TO FOCUS," MATT SAYS. "You just said the things you write in your notebook are silly?" He's speaking with his slimy voice, the one that makes me feel stupid. "Why do you feel these things are silly?"

I shrug. "It just is—the stuff I write without concentrating is silly." It just slips out, falls out. And this is a test. It's always a test.

"But you don't think all your writing is silly?" His voice always gets more high-pitched at the end of questions, and it annoys me.

"No," I say. Because he knows that the writing in my room is the stuff I *really* feel. Because that's what I'm instructed to do, let my feelings out, there. But of course he's still looking at me with that stupid waspkeeper's face, so I have to spell it out for him. "When I write out my feelings, it's real. But these stupid notes I've done in this notebook"—I tap it—"are silly."

"And what do you feel?" Matt asks.

Stupid. Stupid. Stupid.

I lean back on my chair. It doesn't move because it's bolted to the ground. "You know what I feel because you've read my notebooks in my room." I know that because I always put them face-up so they're at a perfect perpendicular angle against the edge of my desk, but every time, when I come back from therapy or Group, the angle is slightly off. Ella, my roommate, always swears it isn't her. And I believe her. The look of terror in her eyes when I first asked her grabbed me like a hand around my throat, made me stop and feel her fear. She's scared of everything.

Matt nods slowly, then he leans back in his chair so the legs creak. His slouched posture reveals another selfie on the wall behind him: him with John Green.

"Okay, so why? Why did you start writing everything down?"

I know he's not just talking about my notebooks. He's talking about me.

I look down at my body, and I see the words covering my skin. Just felt-tip markers. Matt wouldn't let me get anything permanent. Maybe that's just as well. *FAILURE* may wash away in a week's time. Then I can be a *SUCCESS*.

Well, that's if Chaos, the voice inside me, isn't tormenting me.

Matt waits for me to speak again. But I don't. My words are already there. On my body. And he knows enough. He can see enough. *FRIGHTENED* and *VULNERABLE* and *MAKE IT STOP*. But *ONCE UPON A TIME* is out of sight.

There's no point in adding these words to the notebooks that they read, writing them twice, making each word doubly as powerful. *HURT* is already on me three times, and I can't get rid of it now because the pen in my hand automatically retraces it every night. I don't want the other words to become like that. To lash and bite me at every opportunity, because each one speaks to me. And some are more persistent than others. Others are happy to be washed away.

But Matt doesn't understand. His body is clean. And he's one of the good ones. He's trusted. I'm *NOT TRUSTWORTHY*. I'm an *UNTRUSTWORTHY*. I'm an *OFFENDER*. My labels are stuck with me. Forever. Written both ways. Labels I cannot wash off. Even if they let me out of here, no one will trust me. It doesn't matter what the trial says; I still did it, I still proved who I am—not just an Untrustworthy but an Offender, too. Oh, the authorities will be pleased to know their Detector Room works.

Yes. Concentrate on that, Chaos whispers. *You were sorted into your group at the age of twelve and two months, the moment the room spat the U word out.*

I flinch.

My body was clean then, when I was twelve.

It is not now.

DIRTY. DIRTY. DIRTY. It's on my arm, the word getting bigger and angrier each time.

And cray-zay, don't forget that!

Shut up, I tell Chaos. I don't like it when she interrupts when it's not her turn. Because we take it in turns—unless I ask her to step in—and she can say what she wants about me when it's her turn. But it's not her turn yet.

Chaos shuts up.

"Come on, Kira. Concentrate," Matt says—only, for a fraction of a second, I think he calls me something else. Not

Kira, but… No. "Why did you start writing everything down? Why can't you say those things aloud?"

And I'm… I'm still in his office. For a moment that is both beautiful and tragic, I'm startled. Don't know where I expected to be, but I stare around in wonder. There are so many eyes on the celebrity wall watching me. Each eye whispers that it's both 2014 and not 2014, because time isn't right here.

"Um," I say, twirling my felt-tip. "Writing things down makes them real, even if they disappear. They're still real for the moment. Still real."

I look at the words on my left arm. I'm left-handed and those words are always harder to write, look more wobbly. LIAR. PIG. BAD.

Matt's eyes follow my gaze. I snatch my arm away quickly, hide it under the desk.

"You're not a liar," he says. "Or a pig. Or bad. You're a person, Kira. A person who has been hurt by an awful individual."

By a society that lets it happen.

I grit my teeth. My people…we're not valued. We have no importance. I was surprised to even learn that this place has people like Matt, people who care about what happens to us. Because the rest of the country, the rest of the world, doesn't care. We're just the bad people. First, I was one of the ones society pushes to the edges, the people who have to move to the Lowers' accommodations when we leave school, the people who live among the rotting rubbish, kept out of sight from all the valued people of society, the Pures.

Then I became worse.

And no one can see it. No one can see, and our society is exactly like the ones in all those novels I read. We're trapped in a living dystopia, and only the Lowers can see it because it's *us* who's oppressed. Everyone else is happy—happy because us undesirables are not allowed in the same part of the world as them, so they don't see the darkness.

No one sees the darkness, but me. But us.

"You have to understand that none of this is your fault," Matt says. "What happened was not your fault."

But it is. My hand itches to rip my shirt off and write on my stomach, because that's the clearest stretch of skin. And I need somewhere to make sense of everything.

"Look at me," Matt says. "It was not your fault. You have to believe that."

NO, I am writing in the notebook again. *I AM A LIAR, I AM—*

"You're not." He doesn't even wait until I've stopped writing.

"I lied to you," I say. "My name isn't Kira. See? I'm a liar."

I look up and for a moment I see *LIAR* graffiti-d across his selfie board. Maybe it is all lies. Photoshops and cardboard cutouts. Maybe everyone is a liar, and the Detector Room just singles out the really bad ones.

Like me.

BAD itches on my foot.

Matt shakes his head. "You're still taking your medications, aren't you?"

I nod. He knows I am. The baddest guard of them all would have told him if I wasn't. She's a horrible woman, and she insists I call her *Matron*. But her job just proves that we're bad; we all have to be drugged for them to even sit in the same room as us. Maybe it's not kindness, after all. Maybe even Matt doesn't care about what happens to me. This is just his job.

"Good." Matt writes something down, then makes a deep sound at the back of his throat, like a dog growling. No, not a growl. Just a…a noise. I don't know the word. And I should. I have a dictionary in my room. I like words.

But I know what Matt's thinking, and I know his *good* is a lie.

I am *BAD*.

That is why they put me in here.

My Sister, Brooke

I LOVED MY TWIN SISTER MORE THAN anything. More than life itself—and I know that's a cliché, because I know a lot about words, but it's true. Me and my sister, Brooke, we'd do anything for each other. The two of us were the closest you can get without piercing our skins with knives, peeling back our layers, and climbing inside each other's brains.

We weren't identical, and people always thought that meant we weren't in sync. But we were, me and Brooke. Brooke was what I lived for. Who I lived for. And she, me. Kira and Brooke, and Brooke and Kira.

Without her, I'm nothing. And no one gets it. No one cared when they found her body with the U burnt onto her forehead. Hers *always* looked angry, like it had only just been done. Mine healed a lot better. Mum didn't know why. Mum didn't like talking about it, how she, a Pure, married to another Pure, had given birth to two Untrustworthy daughters. After our Detector Room results, Mum didn't go out with the other mothers as much. She said they all grouped together, going to places for Pures. And Mum could've gone, because our results didn't affect who she was, but she didn't. Sat at home with us instead. Watching *EastEnders* and *Countdown*.

She never blamed us, though. Dad might've, but Mum didn't.

But Brooke wasn't bad. The detector room said she was an Untrustworthy, but she never lied. She never deceived anyone.

Not like me. Even if I only became this way because of the events that led to Brooke's death. Events that started way before I was anywhere close to finding out what was going on.

And I should've done something different about it. I know that now.

Brooke is dead because of me.

Routine

*THE GUARDS LOCK YOU UP LIKE CLOCKWORK,
Kira. Interrogation. Group. Social mingling—which isn't really
social mingling, rather it is them just forcing you together with
more Untrustworthies in the common room that you all call 'the
attic,' though you do like Jase and Gav and even Maria—and
then dinner and back in the cage.*

*If I sit back and let your autopilot take over, then you eat only
a little because you know your stomach can't be full as you need
to be clever. You've been looking to escape—or at least you have
when I'm in control, and I'm still you—and so I had you eat
some of the up-to-the-mark food, at dinner. Protein. Vegetables.
No carbohydrates, because people who escape these places are
always slim in the movies—you know, the movies you like.*

And to be sure you fit the image, that you look the part when we eventually get out of here, you do one hundred push-ups at the foot of your bed. Your chest shudders, and your heart pounds but you feel pride when you've done it. Because you're strong.

You're so strong when I'm in charge of your body, and I'm making you better. So much better.

At nine o'clock, the guards come. They give you the sleeping pills and watch you take them. But I hide them under your tongue and stash them away under the rug when they've left. There's quite a collection there now since I took you over in the evenings, because it's important.

You need to get out.

You're in danger.

Next week, they're doing the assessments again. A test to prove your Untrustworthiness. To prove you are who the first brand says you are.

They can't afford to keep everyone here. You're the lowest of the low.

And that's why you're going to escape, very soon. You've just got to sit tight in the times when I'm not here. And I know you won't remember this, not during the times when I've stepped back, but I need you to, Kira. Because they'll tell you things.

They'll say you're ill, that you're traumatized, delusional, that they're helping you, and this is a hospital.

But it's not.

They're the enemy. They're weeding out the citizens who have become Offenders.

And they're going to kill you.

And if they kill you, they'll kill me, too.

But I'm a survivor, Kira. So, you have to be, too.

My Secret Voice

I LIKE HAVING CHAOS INSIDE MY HEAD. She is the voice only I can hear, and she has been my biggest comfort for a long time. Even when Brooke was alive, that final year especially, my sister had changed. She withdrew—and it's obvious now why she did. Don't get me wrong, I still would have done anything for her, but I needed a close friend, too, for the times when Brooke was too shut off from me. And Chaos was here.

This is her body too, now, has been ever since she arrived with me—I'm not sure when exactly that was, but it was maybe a year before Brooke died. And before Chaos was with me, she was with Brooke. I don't know how Chaos got trapped in my body. She said she'd been floating around ever since she'd been released from my sister's body—and she found herself drawn to me. She described it like magnets. She couldn't stop the pull.

We talked a bit, at first. Little snatches of conversation, here and there, and then bigger snatches of information, with Chaos slowly telling me what I needed to know, before we came to our arrangement.

And now it's the two of us.

Chaos and I don't always get on, but I trust her. I know she has my back, just as I have hers. She may not have a body, but we share mine, and that's plenty for both of us.

She takes over and later narrates to me, so I know what I do in those times when I am not me. And then it's my turn again, because it makes her tired.

She says it's been a long time since she had her own body.

Truth or Lie

"HOW DO YOU KNOW THAT ANY OF THE STUFF I said to the police that night was true? And at the trial? When I can't remember it? I could've said anything. I lie all the time."

Another session with Matt. They're endless, each one seamlessly blending into the last. But that's what happens to all the sessions and days here. It's an endless reel, and it's on a loop.

At first, when I arrived here, fresh with my O branding to match the older U carved into my skin, I tried to count the days. Tried to keep a calendar, keep organized, just as I knew Mum would be expecting me to. Dad never cared about being organized, but Mum did, and I hung onto that—the idea that if I kept myself organized in prison, I'd at least be partly redeemed in Mum's eyes.

But I couldn't keep my calendar. The woman who makes me call her Matron took it away. I counted three days and nights, and then I got angry, and I can't remember why, but they put me into isolation—a room with no windows, a bright bulb, and a locked door. Only the same constant light level and the flashing red of the camera in the corner. In isolation, I had nothing to mark day and night. Even the meal times changed each day—there was no routine, and I hated that. Hated eating my food in the same artificial light, when really, I needed the darkness.

Matt places his fountain pen down carefully. A little ink bleeds out onto the soft pad of white paper. I wonder if the ink will bleed the same into the white cotton of my tote bag that rests on my lap.

"Forensic evidence supported your story," he says, gently. "And the detectives found further evidence in the offender's house, linking him to you and two other students. One of the other victims was also able to give evidence. We know you're not lying. We know you suffered greatly. And we know that none of this is your fault."

But he's wrong.

I am Untrustworthy. Right from that very moment, UNTRUSTWORTHY was all I could be.

The Detector Room

WE WERE TWELVE WHEN SOCIETY NOTICED US, me and Brooke. Standing in line, waiting our turns, hurting not a hair on anyone's head. The teachers were so excited their excitement was tangible—disgusting to show that much emotion. It was a thing I could reach out and grab and squeeze, like the shiny insects I now see a lot of the time, in the hope that droplets of their excitement would reach me. But it didn't happen. It was just for the teachers, that pure excitement. Not us.

Well, the teachers *and* the parents. But we pretended we were a bit excited, too, not just nervous, because The Detector Room would, very shortly, read us all, and it would tell us everything that we needed to know.

I've always liked knowledge, liked knowing things. The facts. Science was my favorite subject at school. Then mathematics. Because they both have right answers. You know when you are right. They aren't like English, where things are open for interpretation, and where the teacher always comes up with another 'right' answer—but how can so many be right?

That was why I should have liked the idea of The Detector Room. It said things how they were. It was certain.

Before me and Brooke, it was our friend's turn. Mallory looked scared as the voiceover asked her to enter the room and for the next candidate—me—to get ready. Mallory was jittery-nervous. But she was *always* jittery-nervous. The teachers gave her reassuring smiles as she walked past them, heading into the lair, and I hoped that a droplet of those smiles would maybe fall on me. It didn't. Nothing for me, as Mallory disappeared through the doors.

The light flashed green a few moments later. Green for Pure. It had been a long line of greens so far, only broken by one blue for Manipulator, two yellows for Egocentrics, and a purple for a Conceited, right at the start. Their parents had looked disappointed with the colors, but the readings were all low enough, even within those sectors, for the children to still live their lives among Pures when they became adults.

They weren't Untrustworthies.

"Kira Taylor," the mechanical voice said. "Please enter The Detector Room. Brooke Taylor, please make sure you are ready to enter next."

Brooke gave me a reassuring smile and hug. "You'll do brilliantly," she said, smiling. The sun was behind her golden hair, and she looked like an angel.

Then I disappeared through the doors.

That was when everything changed.

Untrustworthy

I WATCH MYSELF FREQUENTLY—WHOLE DAYS recalled in the blink of an eye. My older self watches my younger self, and I watch that particular memory a lot. The Detector Room. That scene. Maybe because it's one I can remember so well. That part where my younger self walks through the door, because she doesn't know what is going to happen.

It was the point of no return. I often think that.

No one else can watch their memories like I can—or, if they do, they don't talk about it. So, I don't either. Not anymore. Not when Monika is trying to find more reasons to justify my oppression. She's Matt's boss, I think. I just tell her I can't remember much about anything, but I'm sure she knows I'm lying.

I don't mean to lie.

But it's in my DNA.

Still, I'm not lying about one thing though.

The Detector Room is a room. It is a room where there's nothing. Nothing that you can see. But it is full of science and The Detector Room reads you like a book, and then it writes its thoughts down and spits you out—*you* being what you are.

For Mallory, it was: `COMPASSIONATE. CLEVER. KIND. LIKELY TO BE A DOCTOR.`

I was jealous. I wanted to be a doctor. But the machine couldn't find a job for me. There wasn't one in me. There never is for people like me.

And one word sealed my fate. And my sister's, too. `UNTRUSTWORTHY.`

And what did they do then?

Chaos knows what they did, but she still asks, and so I still answer her, in my head—she wants me to think about it and there must be a reason for that. Think about the red-hot metal sizzling against my forehead as they burned the letter U into my bleeding skin. I listened to my screams, swallowed them, spewed them.

And then?

Then the Bad Stuff started, and when it stopped, my sister was dead, and they sent me to the De Hewitt Facility for Offenders. Can't have me causing any more danger in the real world.

The Bad Stuff

THE BAD STUFF IS BAD.

Very bad.

It got worse.

It follows me, though I can't remember it all. Not really.

Not all of it.

But I know more than Chaos told me, more than she thinks I know, and she knows more than I do about some of the parts. It's strange—we talk to each other. And when she takes over, I don't hear everything. Just bits and pieces of what's going on, sometimes, if I'm trying. Like a narration that I'm only half-listening to. She gives me summaries now though, at hand-over. But she didn't then.

Chaos wants to protect me, and she thinks she is.

But I remember the sounds. Some sounds. From that night.

Brooke's last gurgled breath.

The slap of my bare feet in the pool of her blood.

The gunshot.

The scream. The woman's scream—except it can't be a woman's scream because it was only me and that man there, alive, by that point. And it wasn't me who screamed. Maybe it was him. High-pitched. It must've been. Because he knew it was over then.

He knew I'd kill him.

I remember the songs at the funeral, also. Even though I wasn't there. I was locked up, and they were adding the O to my forehead, next to the U, marking me. UO. I wish they'd put some sort of punctuation between the two letters.

No, think of the funeral.

Yes. I'm getting distracted. Sorry, Chaos.

The funeral, right.

I can tell you what Mum was wearing (the lovely floral dress that she wore to my christening—I can tell you about my christening, too, which doesn't make sense, but like I've said before, time isn't right here, it's confusing, so many things at once, and now I know things from before the Bad Stuff was happening, like, *way* before, but that might be because Chaos is with me too now). And I can tell you which aftershave my father used (the horrible one that makes him smell of pine and disinfectant). I can tell you how the casket was closed and how some grieving woman wanted it open, how this old aunt ran up to it and tried to pry the doors off with her long-nailed claws.

I wasn't there, yet I know the things that happened. The details.

But people don't really want to discuss those details with me. They just redirect me into talking about myself, about how *I* feel. I don't know why they do that. Because they know I'm going to lie. It's written on me. They know I'm Untrustworthy and an Offender.

But in a strange way, I like the U. It's like the words I write help me—because I didn't really start writing before The Detector Room detected me. And my words cover me. They're my thick skin. They protect me.

They keep the people away.

Maria

"DID YOU SAY ANYTHING?" MARIA ASKS ME. Her eyes are narrowed, and she accuses me with her face. She does that often, and I know she's accusing me of being with Gaz as well. Not just of telling on her.

We're not allowed relationships here. Untrustworthy Offenders aren't allowed to do things that can breed more Untrustworthies and Offenders, and we're encouraged to report on each other. Every time Matt calls me in to talk about the Bad Stuff and my feelings and my words and my memories—those sounds and the aftermath that floats in my ether—Maria thinks I'm tattling on her.

As if I'd be stupid enough to do that.

Two weeks ago, Maria dodged having her medication for several days. I don't know how it happened—whether she slipped by unnoticed or pretended to have it and spat out the round, white tablets later—but everyone knew within a few hours on Tuesday morning. That's when it built up. She was screaming, running around, and had grabbed a knife from the kitchen, even though we're not allowed in there and there are plenty of guards to prevent that sort of thing happening. Not that it did that, prevented it. She got the knife anyway.

"I'll kill you all, I'll kill you all, I'll kill you all," she screamed, feral.

Or maybe I imagined that.

I'm not sure. I imagine a lot of things—like insects, shiny. Or rather, they *say* I'm imagining them. But they're real. Very real. As real as Maria's delusions, for she is fixated upon the idea of killing. Good job that The Detector Room noticed that in her. Society was already keeping an eye on her, before she came here.

We all know Maria's going to kill someone, too, one day. I already have her bite mark on the back of my right arm. Or, at least I think I do, because now when I look for it, I can't find it and—

"Kira?" Maria snarls.

I shake my head.

"Ah, you're not mute again, are you?" She scowls at me. But at that moment, a guard comes up.

He's one of many guards stationed in the attic, watching us. They try and blend into the walls, mostly, until they don't. This guard is not a guard we like—too big and burly—and his upper lip curls as he takes in me and Maria.

"Time for your crazy pills," he says to Maria.

"You calling me crazy?" she asks, her voice rising. "Really?" And then she's shouting, screaming, swearing, and honestly, he should know better. The Detector Room may have picked up on the instability or something in Maria, as she told me, that led her here, and she may use that word for herself—"I'm just so crazy I can't live out there"—but on her lips it's reassuring, it's *her*, it's *us*; on his it's a weapon.

Maria screams and screams, and then he takes her away. She's all kicking and screaming and wild blond hair, until she's gone, then she's nothing.

I wander slowly to the common room. More chairs bolted to the floor. We're mostly Untrustworthy *and* Offenders—we might try and bash someone's head in with a chair if we could. Even the table is bolted down, too.

It's boardgame-night. Fun.

Jase sees me and then comes over, takes my hand, and leads me to the table in the corner. He's been doing this a lot recently, and I don't understand what it means.

It means he likes you!

No. I freeze. No one can like me.

I won't let them.

"Did they get you to talk about the Bad Stuff?" Jase asks.

He asks this many a time, and he's meaning the stuff that brought me to The Facility, but he asks it in a way that isn't pushing. Everyone here knows about the Bad Stuff—or at least they know I killed the man who hurt me.

But something else happened that night, too.

I get my notebook out of the tote bag that I remember is on my shoulder, and I turn to a new page. A crisp white page. Usually, I use and reuse the same page, writing at many different angles and in many different colors, over and over previous messages and thoughts, until the whole page is the mass of words that is me.

THEY TRIED, I write. But these words look lonely. I stick my tongue out slightly as I think.

"But you're not ready?" Jase asks. He looks over his glasses at me.

NO. NOT READY.

Then I look at the page, and I'm annoyed that it's no longer new. It may not be marked like my body, but it's still marked. Still not clean. I feel the anger rising in me like a tide, rougher and rougher, so I transfer those words from the clean page of the notebook to my right arm. NOT READY NOT READY NOT READY.

Then I rip the page out, and half of me wishes I could rip my arm out of its socket too. Screw it up, discard it, leave it in a trash can.

Jase's eyes are wide. "Your notebook," he says.

I shrug. It's the first time I've ever ripped a page out of one of my notebooks. I'm not sure why I did it, now. Maybe that was Chaos, taking control of me?

Jase tenses, opposite me, and his big brown eyes brim with concern behind his lenses, barriers. I often think of glasses as barriers. Or waspkeepers.

"Are you okay?"

I nod.

"You'd tell me if you weren't?"

I nod again, very aware that two guards have moved closer and are watching me. I stare at the crumpled paper in my hand. Have I displayed too much anger? What if the guards think it's a sign of another violent outburst—a murder? What if they decide I'm not curable and that I don't deserve a place at The De Hewitt Facility? What if they evict me and send me to the place where Incurables go? Or worse, to the Lowers' accommodation…with more men like *him*.

I quickly smooth out the paper. NOT READY looks more savage than the other words.

"I played tennis earlier," Jase tells me. I know he's trying to help—if he can engage me in a normal conversation and I can show the guards that that wasn't really a display of anger, they'll let me stay here. Won't they?

I give Jase the look that means 'go on,' and he tells me all about the match he had with Winston. I can't remember who Winston is.

I'm glad that Jase is here. Of all the Offenders at this prison, he's the one I like the most. Him and Maria and Gaz. We're friends, sort of, the four of us. But Jase and I are *best* friends. Maybe it's because he's here and even when I couldn't speak at all, he was still patient with me. And now, even though I can speak—sometimes—he doesn't push me to speak all the time. Not like Maria. She gets annoyed with me.

"Why can't you just speak like a normal person?" she often says.

WHY WHY WHY, screams my skin, just thinking about her words.

I grit my teeth. I need punctuation.

I add the marks in.

WHY? WHY! WHY.

There, that's better.

I Eat at Night

ONCE JASE HAS FINISHED TELLING ME ABOUT his match, I play boardgames with him for the last hour of free-time. Then it's dinner and phone calls. I stare at the cold macaroni and cheese on my plate. I can't bring myself to put a forkful in my mouth. Not with them all watching.

And it's carbohydrate! Come on! You can't eat that! Protein and vegetables, that's what you need.

I stiffen. Chaos. I don't know how she does it. She can so easily talk to me when I'm in charge. But when we swap, when I give her complete control, I'm just... I'm often just gone. Swallowed. Like I never existed. Can't infiltrate her narrative. She's careful about that.

I stare longingly at the macaroni and cheese. Wonder if I could take it to my room, eat in secret.

But I'd still know. And you shouldn't eat that shit.

My stomach gurgles as I leave the dining hall, along with everyone else. I pass Monika, and I know she is watching me and probably knows about my violent outburst earlier.

Oh, come on, Kira, that wasn't even violent. People screw pages up all the time.

I tune Chaos out—or maybe she fades away because she knows it's not her turn. This is my time.

Monika shakes her head in a sad way and asks if I wasn't hungry tonight, and I tell her I wasn't, but I know she'll bring me food to my room later. She often does. But Chaos is in charge in the evening. I don't have to think about the mechanics of eating. Chaos sorts it, for me.

It's better that way, to eat alone, at night, hidden away. People can't see then that I—an Offender and an Untrustworthy—am eating valuable resources. There's barely enough food left in the world. Not since the Second Bang. It's one of the reasons why The Detector Room was brought in. People who can contribute more to society are entitled to more food, better food.

My mouth waters for chocolate, and I know that even if Monika brings a bar, I'll have to refuse it. Just like I had to with the cake, on my birthday. She'd even written '17' on it, tried to care about me even though she didn't know me because I'd only been here for what, three weeks then? But she knows me now and she shouldn't try and tempt me, because I know she's trying to trick me. Trying to get me to accept what isn't rightfully mine. And then she can say I'm a thief, and I'll have to write THIEF on my body, too. My skin must be accurate.

I sigh, and I think of how different my life could've been.

So, I switch to my other body—the body in the world I *can* control—and I tell myself a story. My favorite story.

My Favorite Story

I LEAVE MY OFFICE AND RETURN HOME. MUM IS waiting for me and is happy to see me. Dad is there, and he's happy too. And of course Brooke is here, happy and alive and not lying in a casket six feet under as her body decomposes. We all hug and we all eat together. I'm not covered in words; my skin is smooth like unrippled water. So beautiful.

Everything is all right here.

Mum asks how my day was and whether I had any difficult patients. Because I am a doctor and everyone's proud of me.

"It was a relaxing day," I say, and I speak loudly and clearly because no Bad Stuff can happen or has happened, and I am **KIND AND COMPASSIONATE AND A DOCTOR.** In this world, Mallory is the bad one who has bad words on her skin. My body is clean.

I look down at my arms now, to check they're clean, because even in this story, I have a memory of when they weren't. But it's a memory from a past life because my arms are good and not even any ghosts lurk in my pores here.

AFTER DINNER, RAVEN ARRIVES TO PICK ME UP. Four minutes early to be precise. I'm impressed—though, naturally, I try not to show it because I mustn't seem like I actually like him, especially not when my parents are waiting with me, and although I'm a doctor and twenty-six years old in this story, they still think I'm innocent.

I'm ecstatic that Raven has turned up. I didn't think he would. I barely spoke to him at school, but he must have somehow received all my secret telepathic messages where I declared my undying love for him.

Okay, that's a bit dramatic, but I love that sort of stuff. I've always wanted to be swept off my feet by a guy wearing a nice suit. And, lo and behold, what is Raven wearing for our date? A tailor-made dark gray suit that's just tight enough around the arms to hint at his biceps.

I'll drool over his biceps later.

My parents answer the door to Raven, and I'm upstairs. I'm looking out the window, and I can see the three of them talking together, just outside the porch.

Then Raven looks up and sees me and gives me that really sexy look that makes my heart melt. (In this story, our hearts are two halves of each other.)

I run downstairs, and then we're holding each other, and I can't think of anything better. Raven's hair is spiked up like a hedgehog and the gel smells faintly of hibiscus. I never normally like hibiscus but now I love it. It's the most wonderful thing in the world.

My parents wave me off, and then I watch my house disappear in the rear-view mirror of Raven's car. Raven has a nice car, an Audi, and he takes me to a secluded place in the woods. Raven has made a picnic, but neither of us eats it.

We stretch out on the tartan rug, and I gaze into Raven's eyes. We're both lying on our sides, our bodies mirror images.

His eyes are the type that swallow me, and I find myself falling into his soul. His soul is the kind of place that puts gates around me and keeps me safe for ever and ever. No one else can get in. And I know that with him is the safest place to be.

"What are you thinking?" Raven's voice is deliciously deep and reminds me of dark chocolate melting over a bed of truffles, the silky texture illuminated by candlelight. The candles are just suddenly here, and they smell of vanilla. Vanilla is now my favorite scent. Vanilla and hibiscus.

"I'm thinking of you," I say, because I am, and saying anything else would be lying, and lying is bad.

Raven smiles.

And now everything is perfect.

Huh, Nothing is Perfect

YOU'VE FINISHED YOUR STUPID STORY, AND IT'S my turn to be here. I'll tell you later what's happened—just the basics though. Not my thoughts. I'm not as open as you.

And now I am you, Kira Taylor.

You are me, and I am you.

Monika brings food to your room because you didn't eat enough earlier. Your stomach is gurgling so much now, and you—read: me—wonder if it's too late for you to eat.

But of course it isn't.

It's no longer macaroni and cheese, but a ham-and-anchovies sandwich. You eat it eagerly.

Monika suggests that tomorrow you'll eat at the same time and place as everyone, and I say you'll try. Though we both know you won't.

She leaves, smiling, and a little while later, a guard comes with the medications.

Your autopilot body wants to take your medication—and it's not just sleeping pills this time either—but of course I have to stop you. It's such a mess when two people occupy the same body. Don't you think so? How do you medicate one without affecting the other?

Ella watches you/me. You've still got half a sandwich left. I give it to her because I've always thought she looks a bit thin. Mickey Mouse wouldn't approve of her thinness—and you—or rather, I—contemplate telling her this, because Ella is obsessed with everything Disney, most of all Mickey Mouse. When you first met her, you thought it would be the princesses with their impossible anatomical proportions that she would love. But no, it's good ol' Mickey. And you're still not sure why he doesn't approve of her thinness, given his Disney princess sisters have the same figures. It should be what he's used to.

But it's not Ella's fault, why she's like this.

You know why she stopped eating the first time, and you turn away to give her privacy in case she wants to eat the sandwich. What a kind girl you are, Kira Taylor—at least, you are when I'm in control.

Ha. Ha. Ha.

I really need to feel more in tune with your body. You. You. You. Me. Me. Me.

I wait until it's a little later heading for the door. It's not locked, but I know there's a sensor on it that detects movement. It'll flash in the guards' office. It does it every time you get up to use the bathroom in the hallway at night. Your bladder has an awful capacity, Kira.

I peer through the little window in the door. No one is out there, though the light is on the lowest of the dim settings. There is no other window in your room, only Ella's drawing of one.

"I'll get us out soon," I whisper, in your voice. "But it's not quite time yet."

Sometimes I'm annoyed that you don't remember the Bad Stuff. Not properly.

Not like I do.

Because I remember everything. And this is eating me alive, because your body is rotting under the weight of it, Kira. And it's not just you who lives here.

Stab. Stab. Stab.

THE NEXT MORNING, I STARE AT THE NEW words in my notebook: HOME. MOTHER. HELP ME. DON'T LET ME DROWN. KILL HIM. IT'S EATING ME. TOO SHARP. STAB. STAB. STAB. STAB.

I grimace. I don't remember writing them, but I know I did it. I do a lot of things now without realizing. And I know I have to be careful. I can't let the guards see these words—these violent thoughts. I have to be alert, even more so after yesterday, and I can't write, *mustn't* write how the badness I feel eats me, how it sharpens and sharpens into little points that *stab stab stab*, because the staff reads everything.

I can't tear another page out, so I set to work with writing new words over the top, try and disguise them.

It's strange. When you write something down, no matter how private it is, people seem to think it's okay for them to read it, no matter what. Especially if it's *on* your body. Especially if you might wash it off in an hour's time, because then it becomes a game, a challenge. They have to read the words—read *you*—while your message is still available, while it's present. Because everything is temporal. Life is temporal. And that's what the men and women here keep doing when they check on me and give me their drugs to make sure I behave, and insist on watching me in the shower so they can see all my words.

I don't shower very often. I don't want them to know all my secrets.

I sprawl out on my bed as I work on the page. There's a camera in the top left corner of the room, and I imagine one of the guards sitting in front of a screen somewhere, watching, checking I haven't killed Ella.

I look across at her; she's sleeping. I wonder if the guards can tell the difference between sleeping and dead on the camera. Not that I'd kill her. I definitely wouldn't see my parents again if I did.

It's been a long time since I saw my parents.

I thought they'd visit. I was sure they would, especially with the trauma and then the trial. I thought it would make them love me again, that they wouldn't then care what The Detector Room had marked me as.

When I first arrived, I spent days and days hovering outside the Day Room where they take visitors, watching the men and women swarming in like insects. No, not insects. A herd of horses. And I'd wait for my parents to be part of the herd. Wait and wait.

WAIT burns on my arm.

They never came.

The guards would watch over me like a hawk when I was waiting. Some would try and talk to me, put on kind faces, but each time Chaos suggested she took another turn, and I was happy to let her deal with it. After, she'd tell me that the guards just wanted me to move on, to not obsess about my parents not coming.

But how can I not? They're my parents.

And they've cut me off.

In telephone hours, I've called our home phone several times. No one answered, and then the last time, a voice—not Chaos—told me that the number had been disconnected. I imagined the line being cut with a pair of very sharp and very big scissors. My parents' line to me. Broken. That snap was the extent they went to, to avoid me. To avoid the shame of not only having two Untrustworthy daughters, but a dead Untrustworthy daughter and a living Offender one.

And maybe the worst part is that I can understand it. Mum's a surgeon. Dad's a councilor. Respectable jobs. Easily tainted if anyone saw them going to the prison. And then no one would want to be treated by them.

It would ruin everything. *I* would ruin everything.

I sigh and roll to the side of my bed and stare at the shallow book-wall between Ella and me. It's three book-spine-widths high. The spines are carefully selected so each group of three is exactly the same height. It was my idea to divide the room; Ella's to use books from the library here.

I count down the minutes until she'll wake up screaming and the men in black will come and haul her away.

Death

IT'S A SUNDAY, AND WE HAVE MORE FREE TIME on Sundays. Most of my day passes in a blur of reading. I like devouring *The Hunger Games,* reading it over and over, and I wish that I was in the arena. I wish I was free. Even if it means I'll die.

Death, Chaos whispers.

But I don't let her speak. She'll be tired anyway. Won't she? And I have to be KIND and COMPASSIONATE, don't I? Those words appeared on my left arm, in wonky capitals, when I was reading. I often write as I read.

And, in the dead of night, on the rare times when it's still my turn to be in control, I write, too. Chaos doesn't often write, but when she does, it has meaning.

I won't let the new words stay long though. I don't deserve them.

It's dark now, and I'm not really sure where the day has gone. Ella's in bed. The camera in the corner of the room winks a green light at me intermittently. I stare at it, and I tell it when to blink and it obeys me.

I smile.

Ella's one of the nicest Untrustworthies I know. And she's not actually an Offender or anything—not like Maria. I often forget that, about Ella. But the guards must have thought it was safer for Ella in The Facility, after something they say happened to her—something I don't know about and Ella doesn't talk about. But they mustn't think that I'm too much of a threat, really. Not when they paired us together. Having her out there, even though all Untrustworthies in the real world are monitored and watched constantly, would be too much of a risk. I'm the lesser of two evils, and The Facility is a safe place.

The guards came for me the day after the Bad Stuff happened. In the night. I can't remember where I was—all I recall is the moonlight kissing branches—but I was somewhere The Facility wasn't, and then I was here, where The Facility is, and Jase smiled at me.

After a while, I fall asleep. Monika doesn't come with any nighttime food, and I wonder if I ate my meal earlier with the rest. I can't remember.

What about the medications? I can't remember that either.

Aren't You Bored of This?

YOU'RE GOING TO BE LATE TO GROUP BECAUSE a guard tells you that Annabel wants to see you first. You don't like Annabel, and if I'm honest, neither do I. Neither of us has since we got here. You don't like her because of her name, and I don't like her because she's one of those people who looks down on those who aren't mentally strong. It's surprising she works here. I suppose it makes her feel superior.

Now, Annabel sits poised at her desk, pen and paper in hand. She thinks she's talking to you—but she doesn't know that 'you' isn't really you today. It's me.

She used to think it was cool, when you first got here, to use her own writing to communicate with you. She said she was trying to understand how it felt to not speak, to rely on the written word. And the first few sessions she stuck to it. But now

Annabel always speaks, ignores the pen and paper in her hands. They're just props. Speaking is less fuss for her. Less effort. She gets paid by how many cases she gets through a day. You were taking up too much of her time when she had to write everything down. They say they've got all the time in the world for us, but they haven't, Kira. You think they should go back to The Detector Room when they lie so frequently, get an updated reading. A more accurate one.

If you were really you, at this point you'd be writing LIAR LIAR LIAR on your arm, while your eyes were fixed on her steel-gray ones.

Annabel clears her throat. What happens is like a script, because there's only dialogue. Though mine is written, because it's funnier that way—to annoy her. I don't write in block capitals like you do though.

Annabel:
The goal, of course, is to get you back into
the world. To get you back out there.

You/Me:
Yes. Get me back into the world. The wild.

Annabel:

We can fit in an assessment for you next Monday—we've got several being done then. That gives us a week. Of course, you won't be going back to your own home so soon, but it'll decide upon the next steps. Your uncle is keen to have you moved back to, uh, yes, there it is—Westward Ho.

You/Me:

Don't forget the exclamation mark—it's named after a book, the only town with an exclamation mark! Did you know that? And I do want to go to Westward Ho! I think it will be really nice there.

(I want that a lot, even though I'm not really sure about your uncle because you never mention him and it's not like he knows you—well, understands you. Or me. Us.)

Annabel:

So you have no problem if I arrange for a new assessment?

You/Me:

No problem. ☺

(I add that smiley face because it's fun to do things you wouldn't.)

Annabel:

Excellent. I really do think you're making great progress.

Still Bad

CHAOS TELLS ME WHAT HAS HAPPENED.

I start screaming.

I can't go to The Detector Room again. I can't.

It's not The Detector Room. It's an assessment. But you're not even going to—

No.

No.

No.

I shake my head.

You're not even going to be here for that assessment! Remember? We're just playing their game, but we're going to get out. And you remember that you need to get out, right? This is a bad place. It's like one of your dystopian novels.

I'm in my room, staring at Ella's bed. I'm supposed to grab my folder and go to Group. But I can't. I can't. I can't.

Annabel's assistant, Raymond, is waiting outside my room.

"I can't go to The Detector Room," I tell him.

Shut up, Kira.

"No, you be quiet!" I hiss. "It's my turn now!" Too late I realize I've spoken out loud, though quietly.

But it's not fair, Chaos sulks. *My turn was only short this time, and you're going to mess things up.*

Yeah and look what you've done, Chaos. I try and send the sentence to her as hard as I can—but it just spirals inside me, and my heart pounds as I stare at Raymond. He's in the doorway now. "I have to stay here. I can't go back to The Detector Room and—"

And he's ignoring me, just telling me, "Come along, Brooke."

Sweat breaks out on my forehead. "That's not me! My sister… I'm Kira."

He rolls his eyes.

Just ignore him, Kira. You know the guards are twisted, think you're all worthless here—they don't mind messing with you. But just ignore what he said, okay? We have to remain strong, make them think we're playing their game. Now, come on. He just wants to take you to Group.

For God's sake, Kira, I'll even do this for you, if you apparently can't.

I feel the anger in Chaos, and it scares me. She's never been angry before. Annoyed, yes. Exasperated, yes. But not angry.

She used to be so nice.

She helped me to tell the stories about Raven, originally, before she got bored of them, thought they were silly. But way back then, when we created the first ones, it was her idea. She knew what Mr. Norman was doing, and it was her way of giving me an escape. Of making my mind go far away, so what he was doing to my sister couldn't really touch me. Not the true part of me.

And she was always there. Chaos was always there to comfort me, to offer kind words.

Until she started getting annoyed.

Only when you started losing your mind. And putting yourself in danger—trying to get the other girl out.

I freeze, and Raymond walks right into me. I scream, turn around and—

"What is the matter?"

I've got a plan, Kira. I'm looking after you still. But you need to get out of here.

No. I'm safe here. I whimper. They want to hurt me out there. Everyone wants me dead. I killed a Pure.

Chaos sighs. *No, listen. Kira, you're getting confused. You remember that you're oppressed here, don't you? And how in those dystopian books the place that seems good and safe is often the worse?*

I nod. Raymond's looking at me strangely, and he's speaking to me, still calling me by my dead sister's name, asking what the matter is.

It's the same here, Chaos says. *You think you're safe here, but you're not. They're trying to keep you confused and forgetful and weak—so they can control you. And they've got all of you where they want you. They're going to hurt you. And you've got to get out. You trusted me before, didn't you?*

Yes.

Then trust me now. I've got a plan. We'll be okay, Kira. You and me. But we've got to get out of here.

My bottom lip wobbles. Get out? I—I can't… Can't do that…can't…

You can. We can. But I need to be stronger. We're getting out very, very soon, okay? But I need to rest. If I rest enough, I can take over your body more for longer. And I need a few days for the plan to work. We've got to get out, Kira, before the evil government puts their plans into place. And we don't want that, do we?

No. We don't want that. I know that.

So, just keep things as smooth as you can. Don't draw any attention to yourself. When they talk to you about the meeting, say you're happy with it. It's our only chance. You have to do this, Kira. Remember, I'm objective. I see things. I see the wider picture. I told you what your parents were wearing at the funeral, didn't I?

Yes.

Then trust me. Now, go to Group. And act normally. I promise everything will be all right soon.

Brooke and the Bad Stuff

CHAOS TOLD ME WHAT HAPPENED TO BROOKE. She told me it all, eventually. And my imagination is vivid, and Chaos was very detailed, so I was able to watch it happening.

"YOU DON'T NEED TO FEEL GUILTY ABOUT this." Mr. Norman smiled, revealing teeth that Brooke hoped would rot very soon. "You're very special to me. You know that, don't you? There's nothing to feel bad about. You're being good—for once."

Brooke hovered two tables away from the chair he was sitting on. Even from here, she could see the way he was sitting, with his knees wide. He always sat like that. Brooke looked away.

Outside, Brooke could see her classmates walking to their next lesson. History. She needed to go, and she started to turn.

"We're not done yet, Brooke."

The U on Brooke's forehead started to burn. Her legs trembled. She stayed where she was, her heart pounding. He wouldn't do anything now. She knew he wouldn't. They were at school. He had been careful, each time before. So careful. And he never did anything *here*. He always took her to his house. Said she had to go. Said he'd hurt her parents and me, if she didn't. Said that if she did do what he wanted, he'd even look into having The Detector Room give her a false reading on the next Testing, so she wouldn't be marked any longer as an Untrustworthy and then she wouldn't have to go the Lowers' site when she left school. He even told her he could do the same for me, if she complied. Keep us sisters together, because sisters should always be together.

"Come here, Brooke." His voice was low. A warning. Something we could never escape from.

Group

EVERYONE LOOKS UP WHEN I WALK INTO Group. Raymond is by my side and makes a dramatic display of sitting down on a too-small-for-him chair, and I stare at his paunchy stomach. As usual, he's wearing barely enough deodorant, and his hair looks like a wig of grease. But now I don't like him even more than usual because there's something about the way he's watching me that reminds me of Mr. Norman. The way he looked at Brooke.

I shudder.

"How lovely of you to join us, Miss Taylor," Karen says, smiling. She's the leader. She always smiles.

I head to the only empty seat. It's next to Jase, and he smiles at me.

Group is for the Offenders who can be healed and redeemed—the ones who the people decide there's still a chance for. Outside, people say that it's only for Offenders whose crimes were things like theft or fraud, but there are a lot more of us here. I don't really know who decides it. Maybe the jurors who were at our trials? I'm not sure. But we're the ones who aren't *past it*.

Maria doesn't come to Group.

Maria is *past it*.

The sessions here are for talking about each of our Bad Stuffs and why we think these things happened and whether we think we made them happen and whether we think they will happen again and what we will do if they do happen again. In general, the staff are nicer to the Group-Goers because we're not complete lost causes. We may get out of here, back to the Lowers' accommodation, each of us with a freshly burnt 'H' on our forehead, so we can wander around block after block filled with Untrustworthies and Egocentrics and Manipulators and Conceiteds who will know that we were once so bad.

Maybe they'll want to hurt us.

My mouth dries. But then I think of what Chaos said—how she thinks I'll be safer out there, away from the bad government of The De Hewitt Facility. The dystopia. And Chaos is always on my side. She helps me. She helps me a lot.

Maybe I do need to get out. She'll hide me, protect me.

"We're just getting started," Karen says, still smiling. I like Karen, because she's mostly always respectful of all of us, but I don't like her as much as I like Matt. "We've got a new girl joining us today." She indicates the short, pretty girl next to her—a girl I hadn't even clocked before. Blond hair. It shimmers. I've always wanted blond hair. "So, this is going to just be a friendly get-to-know-you session."

Introductions. That's what that means.

I used to hate introductions, before I came here. Because everyone knew what I'd been marked as, what I was, the moment they saw me, they didn't care for me to tell them my name after they'd seen the U on my forehead—didn't even want to speak to me in case it was contagious.

It's not contagious.

Prejudice is contagious.

"How about you, Mr. Green?" Karen says. "You can start."

Jase rubs his hands together. "I'm Jase. I'm an Untrustworthy Offender." He indicates his forehead, and I stare at the brand there. It's healed quite well. Looks very uniform, neat. "I'm here because I broke the law by refusing to move to a Lowers' site once I was old enough, and I tried to stay living with my parents."

A menial crime. Nothing compared to me. Nothing compared to the darkness in me—a different type of darkness to that which lurks in Maria, who one day will kill someone and laugh.

I can see my darkness; it has eyes, big, shiny eyes that watch me. It's like one of the insects that hangs around me, but this one has cartoon eyes. And it's everywhere. The insect moves so fast, bringing its darkness with it, touching people, infecting them.

And it's me. I am the insect.

Soon, the tendrils will wrap around Jase.

I will be around him, my arms making a cage he cannot escape from, trying to infect him, give him my Untrustworthiness too, even though he is already like me, even though the Untrustworthiness isn't contagious…but maybe it is.

Because I'm a liar.

And what if everything I've told everyone so far isn't true? How would one even know? Because sometimes, when I wake up in the mornings or when I'm waiting to hear from Chaos, to see if it's her turn yet, I feel it. Feel a sense of wrongness. Displacement. And badness.

Like nothing's real, nothing here.

Yet it is, and I don't understand. It's all so confusing.

But my words are bad.

So bad.

LIAR. LIAR. LIAR.

Karen nods at Jase slowly. "But you're doing really well, aren't you? You've shown remorse for your actions and soon The Detector Room will be ready for you again."

He looks happy, for Karen's sake. But I can see through his smile. I can see his own insect in there. Smaller than mine.

"How about you, Miss Taylor?" Karen turns her chirpy voice toward me.

My insect opens his eyes wider, until the whole of each eyeball is visible and each is a perfect sphere of day and night. Then one pops out of the socket and rolls toward me on the floor, leaving behind a milky trail.

I stare at it, aghast.

Then I swallow hard, and the insect disappears. "I'm Kira. I'm here because I murdered someone."

Wrong! You're mainly here because you tried to end your life.

I flinch at the sudden power of Chaos—and she's supposed to be hiding, resting, sleeping!

The new girl looks startled.

"But it wasn't *you*," Karen quickly says. "You were just there. You were not responsible for that man's death."

Maybe that's what I told them. Told them all.

But I'm still here.

And I still remember the weight of the gun in my hand.

Chaos knows what I did. What we both did.

Revenge is important.

I'm sweating. I can feel it dripping down my back. Feel it running everywhere, and everyone must be able to see it. It'll look like I wet myself, that puddle on the floor.

My heart rate speeds up, and I feel it more. It is a countdown getting faster and faster.

And when it stops, that's when it'll all be over.

Escape

IT IS OVER. I AM RUNNING. HALLWAYS AND corridors. Walls and carpet and doors and windows. My insect has reproduced quickly, and the swarm is chasing me.

Or protecting me.

And what if it all is a lie? What if I'm a lie?

And I am.

My name isn't Kira.

It's Brooke. No, that's not right! That's my sister. So, what is my name?

Annabel… The name floats at me, but no, that's wrong. Not my name.

MY NAME. MY NAME. MY NAME. Burning on the inside of my wrist.

I don't know what my name is. But it's not Kira.

I don't actually know who Kira is.

Calm Down

I RUN AND RUN AND RUN. MY HANDS ARE claws and they tear posters off the walls. Angry faces and words that chase me around rounded corners, across the open-plan units, and round and round and round. Never-ending spirals, and ceilings that are too high.

Calm down. Calm down. Look, Kira. I told you to stay calm.

I'm not Kira. It's a lie.

Just breathe. You can't do this to yourself, not again. And you need them to think you're better. We've got to get out.

But I'm not better. My breaths are ragged, burning. The lies are getting bigger.

You think they're getting bigger. But there's a difference. A big difference.

Now, hold on, okay, Kira? When we actually get out of here, I'll take over, okay? But I may need to be in control of our body—well, your body—for days. And I need to get enough power to do so. You understand, right? You have *to be strong now so I can sleep—then I'll be strong enough.*

I don't want to do this.

You haven't got a choice. It's too dangerous here. Just make them think you're recovered, okay, try and make the escape as easy for me as you can.

All Right, Chick?

MONIKA IS ANGRY BECAUSE SHE'S HEARD I RAN out of Group and caused disruption. I want to write that this means I'm NOT HEALED and that I have to stay here. No point going to The Detector Room. Using up their resources on a test I'll fail.

And when they realize I have to stay here, Monika will sigh, but she'll be nice to me. She'll still bring my food to me at night.

Only I don't say that I'm not healed and that I have to stay here when Monika calls me to her office, because Chaos's words ring in my head, and now I look up and see the cameras. I knew that they were there, but not truly that they're watching me. Twenty-four-seven surveillance. These people know everything. There's nowhere to hide. The cameras are everywhere. It's like *Nineteen Eighty-Four*, except it's happening now.

So instead I tell Monika that I ran out because Raymond looks like Mr. Norman. And I didn't like sitting in the room with him watching me.

Monika makes a *hmmmm* sound under her breath. "There will be people out there who look like Mr. Norman. You know that."

"I want to get out of here," I say, and I look at the camera. There must be one in Matt's office too. But I can't think where it is. Unless it's disguised in the eyes of one of his celebrity selfies. I shudder. Maybe it's Leticia Dean. I never did like Sharon in *EastEnders*, when I watched it.

"That's what we want, too," Monika says. "And you will, with time."

TIME. TIME. TIME.

I go to my room when Monika excuses me. Ella's not here, and the door is to be left open in the day, but I lie on my bed and dream of white coats and lots of discussions between the white coats and my uncle, Glenn, about care plans. I don't really know why I think of him. Glenn wanted nothing to do with me the moment The Detector Room spat me out, so

I'm not sure why the white coats are talking to him. Why I imagine this.

I wake up and the U on my head is throbbing. The clock tells me I haven't been asleep for long and—

There is someone in my room.

I jump up, heart pounding, feel adrenaline coursing through my system.

Maria stands by the drawing of a window that Ella did. I watched Ella do that drawing and pin it up next to her bed, because at her home she says her bed is next to the window. She wants this room to be more homely.

"All right, chick?" Maria's voice is scratchy. "You sleep at strange times, girlie." She emphasizes 'girlie,' so it sounds like a bad word and makes me feel like I'm biting down on an impossibly thin piece of velvet.

I nod slowly, then she's stepping toward me, her long legs striding over the wall of books between my bed and Ella's. Ella won't like that Maria was on her side of the room.

"Any new words?" Maria grabs my right arm and turns it over in her slender fingers. Her touch is almost scalding. "*Blemish* and *die*," she reads. "Interesting."

I try to pull my arm away, don't remember writing those words. But they're there. *BLEMISH* and *DIE*. My words. In my writing. My capitals on my skin.

"Matron ain't going to like seeing that," Maria says. "You should cover it up. Here." She grabs one of the felt-tips from Ella's desk where she keeps her artwork supplies—only pens and chalk—and scribbles over *DIE* before I can do anything. She presses hard with the pen, but of course it doesn't hurt. Felt-tips are the only ones we're allowed in here.

I think of Matt's fountain pen in his office. I want to write with that. For once, I want to pierce the paper and watch it bleed.

Blemish and Die

"I'M NOT SURE WE SHOULD BE DOING THIS," I say to Maria three hours later, when we're crouching in the courtyard, outside the canteen's window. The clink of glass and the clatter of silverware drifts through the open window. The staff are busy, and amazing smells curl toward me.

"Oh, relax," Maria says. "You said you were hungry."

Yes, I had said that. Because I didn't eat lunch earlier. But even if Maria and I manage to steal some food now, I won't be able to eat it until it's dark.

"But Monika would get me some food," I point out. "If I asked her."

Maria pulls a face. "And where's the fun in that?"

She stands up, looking over the windowsill, and I stay where I am, hunkered down, my back against the brick wall.

I stare straight ahead, at the rest of the courtyard. We're not allowed out here unless a guard is also with us—and breaking the rules is not something I want to do.

A second later, Maria crouches back down. "Okay, there's no one in this section of the kitchen now. They're farther up—the kitchen's a T-shape, remember? If you give me a leg up, I can climb through the window, grab some food for you, and get out."

It appears I have no choice. I feel sick as I give Maria a leg up, and she disappears. She doesn't even make a sound as she climbs down, or as she lands on the tiled floor. Is it tiled? I don't know. But then I hear Maria's foraging through something to the right of the window, and when I lift myself onto my tiptoes, fingers hanging onto the windowsill, I see her reflection in a mirror on the other side. See her checking behind her.

My heart pounds.

Nearby, a woman shouts something about turning the oven off.

"Hurry up," I whisper, peering through the open window.

"Relax, chick," Maria calls back. Laughing.

She's laughing.

A cool breeze presses against the back of my neck. *Punishment*, the breeze whispers.

Punishment.

My fingers itch to write the word, and I reach down to my pocket. The felt-tip is poking out.

I pull it out, but my hand shakes as I write it below the blacked-out mess that Maria did. But I can still see *DIE* underneath. Even though it's *BLEMISH AND*—

And what? That's what people are going to ask.

Punishment. Punishment. Punishment.

I take a deep breath. I'm shaking.

It's a Prison, Chick

"HEY, CHICK!"

I look up at Maria's shout, see her slender leg stretching out the window, followed by a hand holding a bulky plastic bag.

"Take it," she hisses. "And help me down."

I take the bag quickly, put it at my feet, then try and help her down. But I'm not strong, and she falls onto me, the sharp point of her elbow digging into my chest.

"Wasn't that fun, chick?" she says as she gets up, then pulls me up, too. She shows me what's in the bag: apples, a packet of licorice, sachets of coffee-shop sugar, and a packet of gluten-free chocolate cookies. Foods we're not Worthy enough to have. "Come on!"

We go to Maria's room.

I've never been in her room before, but it looks the same as mine. Except the second bed is empty. She has no roommate.

"Wish you were my roomie," she says as she tears into a packet of sugar.

I watch her, my eyes wide, as she empties the contents into her mouth. A whole packet of sugar. She closes her eyes, bliss.

"Doesn't that make you feel sick?"

"Only one thing makes me feel sick, chick," she says.

A guard walks past the doorway and looks in at us. We're sitting on her bed. The bag of food is behind the bed, and looking at Maria you wouldn't know there was a whole sachet of sugar in her mouth. I imagine it dissolving into her saliva, pooling into a thick, saccharine mess, and my stomach twists. Spots of white light dance in front of my eyes.

"Wanna know what it is?" Maria asks once the guard has gone. "That makes me feel sick?"

I nod slowly.

"These walls. This place. It's a prison, isn't it, chick?"

"It is," I say, and I know Chaos thinks it too, even if she's sleeping right now.

"And you'll get out, chick. But I won't." Maria snaps her fingers. "And that's what makes me feel sick. They're never going to give me a chance. They think I'm just inherently bad."

I stare at the U and O on her forehead. They're both like mine. We're both marked as the same, yet she's different. I am the only murderer, because she didn't succeed. She plotted to kill six, but then she handed herself in. She calls that her *moment of weakness,* when she panicked and told someone her plans. I don't know what to call it.

"Not fair is it, chick?"

"Not fair," I say.

Then I write NOT FAIR on my arm. Right next to BABY MONITOR, those words I pretend aren't there, and I don't know why those words are there anyway. That's not part of my story.

Then Maria shows me what is under her jacket, tucked in the pocket.

She gets it out slowly, revealing the whole object to me so there's no mistaking what it is.

My mouth dries.

A knife.

Maria smiles wickedly, and I see the words hovering next to her, in the air. KILLING MAKES EVERYTHING BETTER. KILL THEM ALL.

No wonder she wants to kill someone when the words are telling her to.

The Knife

I CAN'T SLEEP, BECAUSE I THINK OF MARIA with her knife.

She shouldn't have it.

Has anyone noticed it's gone from the kitchen? They should've, wouldn't they? Won't they?

They will. They will. They will.

THEY WILL.

My heart beats faster and faster. I turn over and over. The duvet cover is crinkly, and there's a waterproof cover under it, around the duvet, beneath the cotton blue cover, and the waterproof cover is rustling. It's laughing at my restlessness. It's laughing and telling me that whomever Maria kills with the knife will die by my hand.

I should've reported her.

And why haven't they noticed the missing knife? Why haven't they counted them?

Why?

Why?

WHY?

I feel sick.

I sit up, stare at Ella's unmoving form in her bed. I try to think which guards are on duty tonight.

But it's not the nice ones, because it's never the nice ones at night. And if they know that I've concealed the crime for this long—hours and hours—they'll hurt me, too. Not just Maria. I'll be an accomplice.

I am an accomplice.

Accomplice to murder.

This is a place for bad people.

I'm bad.

Ella stirs next to me. I freeze, hold my breath—but there's a raging gulf inside me. My fingers shake. They are sticks of ice. A peculiar feeling swims around my stomach, faster and faster.

Tell a story. That's what I need to do, yes.

A story.

I close my eyes.

Kira's New Story

Raven and I board the plane.

We're going on honeymoon—no, holiday.

We're already married. Have been for a while. I look at the wedding ring on my left hand. It's proof. Proof of our love. A huge diamond.

I'm wearing a long, floaty dress. It's mustard-yellow. Raven is wearing jeans and a hoodie. It's hot. He's sweating.

It's stuffy in the plane. I don't like it.

So stuffy.

We take our seats.

I am across the aisle from Raven. I'm next to a woman with a baby. The baby sleeps peacefully the whole flight, and the woman tells me how relieved she is, that she thought her son was going to be a nightmare.

Lots of people are nightmares, I think as I get off the plane.

Raven and I collect our luggage. My suitcase takes far longer to appear than his, and as I wait, I turn my phone on. There's a text from Brooke. She's looking after my cat. I have a cat. I still have a sister. Brooke says the cat is fine.

Raven and I are in Palma de Mallorca, and neither of us speaks Spanish or Mallorquin.

People walk around us, bump into us.

We're statues in the middle of a busy street.

I don't like it.

But it's our holiday. So, it's going to be good, because we're safe and we're Pures, and my sister is still alive, and back home, I have a cat.

Wink, Wink

I OPEN MY EYES, AND—

The knife is in my hands.

Maria's knife.

My breath comes in short, sharp bursts. My vision wavers a little. What the hell?

I look around. It's dark, but there's a little light that allows me to see, and my eyes adjust quickly. Shapes begin to emerge.

Maria's room. She's asleep.

The red light of her camera winks at me, lights up the knife's blade in blood.

What? Blood?

I frown, my brain numb.

I shouldn't have the knife.

I run.

A knife could be useful for whatever Chaos's plan is.

Not an Ordinary Day

WHEN WE WERE FOURTEEN, THE BAD STUFF started.

It was just an ordinary day. Well, for an Untrustworthy. And maybe it was Brooke's label—the U on her forehead—that made him do it (because that's what all the therapists here have said when I have spoken about it). And they must be right. Because no one would've believed Brooke at the time if she'd told them what was happening. She was marked as a liar. Forever made sure that no one would believe her. Believe any of us.

He even said that. He knew what he was doing.

And I think other people knew. Brooke thought that, too.

It makes sense.

He only picked out the Untrustworthies for his special services. It was only the Untrustworthies in his class who had to come back at break time. Only them who he gave detention to when they'd done nothing wrong. Maybe that's because we were bad. Because we lied and cheated on our homework, copying our friends' writings and then saying it was our own work.

And it should've been me, too. I was supposed to be in that class with Brooke. Two of us. I should've protected her. But I wasn't there. I was too good at solving equations. Got moved up to a more advanced mathematics class at the beginning of the year, even though I hated the subject.

I left Brooke behind, left her to endure those classes with him.

Chaos told me about it, but not at first. Not until two years had passed.

But I found out.

TRUTH. It's written on my back. Too small, too late.

IT WAS JUST AN ORDINARY DAY, THAT FIRST DAY when he called Brooke back. When he said she needed detention because she'd copied Mallory's work. And Mallory, sitting next to Brooke, had looked at her in disgust. That was the last time she sat next to any of us Untrustworthies. Her mother called in after that, told them that even though we used to be friends, she didn't want her daughter sitting next to an Untrustworthy, and really, didn't Mallory need to be in a much higher-grade mathematics class? She was going to be a doctor, after all.

Brooke hadn't done anything wrong. Brooke hadn't copied her work. But an Untrustworthy has no place to say that.

There were other Untrustworthies in that class, too. Two of them. A boy called Raven—the boy that Chaos and I tell stories about—and a girl called Fiona.

Raven spoke to me once. Just once. A break time, I can't remember when. Chaos says it was shortly after Mr. Norman started hurting Brooke, but I can't fit that break time into the timeline as easily as I can other things when I'm piecing everything together. Because it was the only time Raven spoke to me, and it feels like it took place in a magical realm. Only in my altered memories.

He came sidling over to me when I was standing alone, waiting for my sister.

The sun was bright, and it reflected off his glasses into his eyes.

"Kira." He nodded curtly, and the action made his dark hair flop forward over his forehead. He immediately dragged it back with his hand—we're not allowed to cover up our brandings. Not allowed to be deceptive. He needed a haircut. I wondered why no one had told him. Taken him to the barbershop.

I stared at Raven.

"Tell Brooke not to go," he said. "After school. It's going to be worse."

"What?"

"Just tell her not to go."

And then he backed away and that was the last time—the only time—I spoke to the real Raven.

But it didn't feel like the last time, and not just because I still tell myself those stories—our stories. The life we should've had. No, his words haunted me all through the rest of break, the rest of the day, until Brooke was standing outside Mr. Norman's office—because detentions weren't in his classroom. Always in his office: second floor, tucked away, empty rooms either side.

Don't go. Don't go. Don't go. And it's strange, because now when I remember it, it's not Brooke it's happening to.

It's me—and it can't be, it really can't be. But it is me who is knocking on the door. And it is Chaos's voice in my head screaming at me as Mr. Norman invites me in.

But that's just wrong.

I already know I am a liar.

The End of the Bad Stuff

IT STARTED WHEN BROOKE WAS FOURTEEN. IT ended when we were sixteen. It ended the day my sister died.

Two weeks later, and I was here. At The Facility. Strange how things happen.

Then I frown. That *was* the timeline. Wasn't it?

And I'm asking Chaos, but she's resting and it's not her turn and she's not even passively listening. No, she's generating energy. I can feel her. She's getting ready. Ready for the escape.

But Raven and Fiona both knew what was happening—because it was happening to them, too. We tried to meet up once, the four of us, toward the end. When Chaos told me what was happening to Brooke, and when Brooke knew that I knew.

"How much longer is he going to be?" Brooke asked. She was looking for Raven.

But Raven didn't turn up.

It was just me and Brooke and Fiona. And the three of us knew, but none of us could say the words. There was something stopping us from speaking—something different, something that hadn't stopped Brooke from telling Chaos to tell me. A hand around each of our throats. I often think I should've had my notebook. That maybe that way we could've talked, and maybe it would've helped.

Instead, we bought Ben & Jerry's ice cream—tubs of Blueberry Cheesecake and Peanut Butter World—and put on a DVD at Fiona's house. A romantic comedy with Jennifer Aniston, because Fiona liked her. It was weird. We weren't friends. But after that day, we did it regularly. Meeting up at Fiona's. The three of us. I even learned her favorite ice cream was mint chocolate chip, even though we always got Blueberry Cheesecake for me and Peanut Butter World for my sister. We couldn't afford a third tub.

Fiona

FIONA'S BRANDING WAS REMOVED A WEEK after we watched that DVD and ate ice cream at her house. She'd been healed. Not in a program, but naturally. By Mother Nature. It happens sometimes. We all had our scheduled Testing appointments—all the Untrustworthies, to see if we'd gotten worse, if we were still safe to remain at a school with Pures—and when Fiona came out, I knew something was different. There were tears in her eyes, but she was smiling.

She said her brain must've healed, because some people believe the Untrustworthies have brain viruses that make us BAD, little bugs that determine our behavior.

But I don't think it's a virus. I don't think my brain is any different. Sometimes, I think it's all a lie. That it's just a random thing whether you get a *BAD* label or a *GOOD* one. Maybe it's all an experiment to see if we live up to labels being placed upon us, just as one of the guards once said happens.

But I am *BAD*.

I've done *BAD* things.

I'm a *LIAR*.

A *CHEAT*.

A *MURDERER*.

And now I've got Maria's knife.

Help

THIS ISN'T REAL. THIS CAN'T BE REAL. I'M holding a murder weapon. Again.

It's not real.

"Are you there yet, Chaos?" I whisper, because maybe if I say it out loud she'll know this really is urgent. I'm risking everything for her to wake up.

But Chaos is sleeping, still. Dead to the world.

My breathing quickens.

I grab my notebook.

And the knife is here. It's real. It's watching me. It's on my duvet. I'm back in my room.

THIS ISN'T REAL. THIS CAN'T BE REAL.

IT'S NOT REAL.

CHAOS?

ARE YOU THERE?????

I DON'T EVEN KNOW WHO I'M TALKING TO. WRITING TO.

I let out a scream.

DO SOMETHING!

HELP ME!

WHY AREN'T YOU HERE?

But writing in the notebook isn't enough. So, I press the ink into my arm. Huge blots that make my words, my tears, my fear.

I DON'T KNOW WHAT THE FUCK TO DO.

Perhaps, the longest sentence on my body. Too many words, and it's unbalanced now, and I flinch. A hollow sensation fills me. Too many words on my arm.

I look at my other arm. The arm. It needs more.

I STILL DON'T KNOW WHAT THE FUCK TO DO.

The Camera

EVENTUALLY, I HIDE THE KNIFE UNDER MY mattress, but I know the camera is recording everything. It's still dark, very dark. The early hours, so the image on the recording might not be good. But it might be too good, hiding no secrets, and—

Calm down, I tell myself. Just calm down.

It's what Chaos would say if she was here.

And what would Chaos have said? When I crept along to Maria's room and got her knife? I can't even remember leaving my room. A fugue state? Or was Chaos awake and controlling me then?

I wait, wait for her to stir. To answer. To help me.

But she doesn't.

It's just me.

I did that. Took the knife.

Because I am *BAD*.

I try to keep calm. The blue numbers on the digital clock tell me that it'll be getting light soon.

And that's when the men in black will come when Ella wakes, screaming. But they'll take me. They'll take me to a prison cell. A proper cell. Not like this one. One like in the movies where there's only a hard metal bed and a chainlink blanket and a metal bucket to go to the toilet in.

I won't have any books there, won't have my laughing duvet, won't have Ella or Jase or Maria. There won't be a Matt with celebrity selfies, or a Monika or an Annabel or a Karen or a Raymond.

No hidden gluten-free chocolate cookies hidden in Maria's room.

"Do you see what you've done?" I say to myself. "Do you see?"

And I'm whispering the words, savagely, wanting them to hurt me, but they don't because they're not real. Because they have no form. They *need* form.

I grab my felt-tip. The lid makes a satisfying click as I pull it off, and, automatically, I look over at Ella, cradled in her Mickey Mouse fort.

DO YOU *SEE WHAT YOU'VE DONE*, I write. Then I add a question mark. And another and another. A whole swarm of question marks, and they're like the insects of life—the insects all around us—that no ordinary person can see.

But I'm special.

They told me that before. *He* told me that.

And he was right.

I can see the insects.

They creep out from under the duvet and crawl over the mattress, over my body, down onto the floor. The carpet is a seething mass of shiny, metal shells and wire legs. The insects are laughing and whispering *Do you see what you've done?* over and over again.

I see what I've done.

And they're going to see.

The knife. I need to move the knife.

It's Maria's problem. Not mine.

But my fingerprints are on it. I gulp.

Slowly, I get out of bed.

The door flies open.

I gulp, jump back and—

"Kira?" Monika's hushed voice.

I nearly scream, but the insects dive into my mouth and stop me. Inside my mouth, they expand and fill the cavity. Their hard shells and soft underneaths press against my teeth and my tongue and the roof of my mouth.

"Are you okay?" Monika whispers, and then she's indicating for me to follow her.

And stern—she sounds stern.

Oh God. She knows.

They all know.

And—and what if they kill me because they think I'm Incurable? Too much of a risk? They must kill us eventually—it makes sense. The Facility has no Incurable Untrustworthies over the age of twenty, I'm sure.

Oh God. I've worked it out. My heart pounds, heavier and heavier. White lights dance in front of me. That's what Chaos was trying to tell me but without using the words, without scaring me. That's why we've got to go.

Monika's speaking to me, and we're out in the corridor, and I don't remember actually leaving my room.

I didn't say goodbye to Ella.

I falter, but Monika tells me to hurry up.

My legs work without me telling them what to do.

"She's in the day room," Monika says.

"She?" I gulp.

The executioner.

"Yes," Monika says. "Your visitor."

I've got a visitor.

I press my lips together slowly as we walk. Monika says my visitor could only visit at this ungodly hour because of work commitments, and the staff agreed to let her in seeing as I've never had a visitor before.

And I—I can't believe it.

My mother.

It's her. It has to be.

I knew she'd come. Knew all along she'd come.

And now she's here.

I can't stop smiling. My smile is so big it hurts my face. It's painful. But it's the good kind of pain.

My fingers itch for a pen. I need to write—write anything, I don't care what. Because she's come to see me. My mother! And now I think of all the words we'll write together, because suddenly my mother's a writer in her spare time, when she's not slicing people open, and she wants to be a writer in her full-time, and she's hoping her new thriller will land her an agent and take off, and then we can both write. Write all the words. Write them all the time.

We can write a new existence for us.

"All the words, all the world," I whisper. "Mum." I roll the word on my tongue, and Monika smiles. My heart aches for the word to be etched over it, forever.

I wonder what my mother will be wearing. Whether she'll have a new designer handbag, and if such a bag would mean she's doing well with her words, because she always said the first thing she'd buy if she got a deal or something would be a new bag. And she loves the one in Debenhams. And if Mum has got a new bag, then maybe she'll bring me a treat.

Jase's parents visit him all the time and bring him sweets and magazines and DVDs—though the guards always confiscate these because they apparently 'promote violence and regressive behaviors.' But his parents bring him books, too. Jase doesn't like reading, so I always get the books—or they're donated to the communal library at The Facility— and the dystopian novels are my favorites. The guards don't think they're a problem, even though they highlight the living dystopia we're in.

It doesn't make sense, really.

But the books are my wall next to my bed, a wall I want to build higher and higher so that the words between me and Ella, me and everyone, grow. A euphoric grin spreads across my face. My mother's words can join them! Join the barrier, make an igloo—an igloo of little black marks printed on cream paper and white paper and bright covers with ornate gold lettering on.

And then I'm running, and Monika isn't here anymore. She went to her office, said for me to go on ahead. And I'm running, and I see the insect—the little, shiny creature following me, and he's been following me since I left my room because he's my anchor.

And the corridors are happy, and it's just me and them and this weird insect.

And now my mother is here—finally!—and she's going to bring me my own books, ones she's written, had published— because she's been busy on a book tour, that's why she's not visited sooner—and she'll give me my own signed copies, and they'll be properly mine. And I will even tell her which books I want to read—who my favorite authors are, after *her* of course—and she'll get these books for me and bring them on her next visit. She'll be visiting regularly now and—

I freeze.

The woman in the day room is not my mother.

No, this woman is too tall. Her face is too thin. Her eyes are too big. Her cheekbones look like they're going to fall off. Fall off and join her husband in the grave. The grave I put him in.

With the maggots and worms.

My mouth dries.

"I've been wanting to speak to you," says Mr. Norman's wife.

Mrs. Norman

I STARE AT MRS. NORMAN, AND ALL THE BLOOD drains from my face, I feel it falling down my body, like every part of me is falling to the floor. And going through the floor, through all the graves and the lands of death, travelling through rock and stone and earth, until I'm at the center of the earth and it's too hot, and the fiery rage tears me into little shreds.

"Take that chair," Mrs. Norman says, indicating the chair opposite her. She smiles. She's wearing lipstick, that bright red shade. The shade that Mr. Norman always painted onto my lips. No, Brooke's lips.

I stare at her lips, feel sick.

Get out. Get out. Get out.

I turn and—

The door's shut. How's the door shut?

Every part of me screams at me to move, to run. But I can't. It's like my body's not my own.

Mrs. Norman's chair scrapes against the floor loudly as she pushes it back. She walks over to me. And then her arm is around me, and I'm shaking. Shaking too much.

She shouldn't be here! Chaos was right—it's not safe here for me. Oh God. I need to get out.

"It's all right, sweetie," Mrs. Norman says. "Come and sit down."

And then she's leading me over, and I'm not resisting, not doing anything but what she wants.

Because that's what it was like and—

My stomach twists violently.

Scream. Scream. Scream. I need to scream.

I sit in the chair, and then Mrs. Norman sits opposite me. She smiles. She's my old English teacher. Of course she is. I stare at her face. I want to grab her face and screw it up like she's just a piece of paper that should've never been written on.

And then I feel it happening: the darkness, the whoosh of numbing poison that spreads and spreads, and it's like the numbness that Chaos would bring me, when she'd whisk me away to tell me my favorite stories.

Only Chaos isn't here.

But the numbness is.

It's okay, I tell myself. I can tell a story.

Chaos told me what to do. Trained me. Gave me an escape.

"It was lovely of them to let me in here," Mrs. Norman says.

I try to tune out her voice. I think of Raven. My Raven. We're in the hospital. I'm lying in a bed. I'm in labor. The contractions are so close together, and a doctor is peering between my—

"They even said it's great when teachers show an interest, that it can really help aid the road to recovery," Mrs. Norman says. "*Aid the road to recovery.* That doesn't make sense, does it? Shit like that never makes sense."

I try not to listen, need to concentrate on the baby I'm giving birth to. But the conditions aren't right—not here and not there. It's too early.

I tremble. I look around. It really is just me and Mrs. Norman here. I think her name is Elaine. But I can't see her as anything more than Mrs. Norman now, because all I can see of her is her husband. There's a photo of the two of them in their bedroom.

Brooke remembered looking up at it when he held her down.

Mrs. Norman places her hands together firmly on the tabletop, then she looks at me and tilts her head sideways. She's wearing a lot of powder and seeing her face painted so white—so empty—against the redness of the lipstick makes the unease in my stomach grow. Grow like it's a worm gorging itself.

"So, how are you doing? You're looking well."

I don't answer. There are no words in me, so I look down at the words on me. At *HELP* on my hand, and I want to write it again and again, like how I used to when I was fourteen. That word became my living thought, my motto, and it was everywhere. I saw it everywhere, and I wrote it everywhere I could.

But no one ever saw it.

Only Chaos, and I don't even know who she is. Sometimes I think she is inside me. Living in my body. But when she speaks, her words sound external. Like she's behind me, speaking. Or in front of me. Not me.

But I know she controls my body at times, and when we swap, she tells me what's happened. She's my friend.

"I must say, you're looking very well," Mrs. Norman says. "Considerably better than, say, my husband."

I make a choking sound as every muscle in my body locks up. I need help. The knife under my mattress flashes into my mind. My throat feels like it's on fire. I need to run, but I can't, my body's betrayed me. Again. It's all my body does. Useless in times when I need to run. And Mrs. Norman once told me how fast she could run. She used to be a sprinter at school. She told the class that once.

The clock on the wall tells me it's ten to six. But Monika's up. She'll come back here, won't she? To check on me? Or the cooks or guards will walk past—the kitchen's not far away. If I wait until I hear the clanging of pans and then scream…

Mrs. Norman leans forward, and her sheet of black hair touches the shiny tabletop, on either side of her clasped hands. "Do you know what your lies have done to my husband?"

Yes, turned him inside out.

Yes, put him in a coffin.

Yes, revealed the monster within.

But they're not lies—are they? Not like she says. Unless I'm…

I inhale sharply, can't help it. I'm confused. Everything is always so confusing now.

"Do you know what exactly you've done to my family? To me? I lost my job because of you. The police implied I was complicit in the…" Mrs. Norman shakes her head. "You've destroyed us, destroyed everything."

I don't understand why she's here, why she's saying these things to me. Brooke told me she and Mr. Norman were getting divorced. That she was leaving him. But I guess his death has changed her mind. She wants to hold onto him. She wants revenge.

I start shaking harder. "Go. Leave." I manage the words, but they're weak. They're nothing. Words spoken are no words at all.

And how did she get in? The guards shouldn't have let her in. They're supposed to protect me, supposed to check everyone.

Chaos was right.

Mrs. Norman laughs. "You want it to go away? Well, it will, for you. You'll get out of here and you'll live your life normally after this." She waggles her finger in the space between us, but she's wrong.

When Chaos and I get out of here, we're going to be on the run. There won't be anything *normal* about our lives then.

I stare at her earrings. But they're clip-ons. No sharp points.

My fingers curl, and my too-short nails feel strange.

"Why are you here?" I whisper.

"To get you to do the right thing." She leans back, and her cold gray eyes flash. "Tell them you lied."

Her lips look too red. Suddenly, they remind me of the chilis that Dad grew when I was nine, and I don't want to associate them with anything of my life. My family.

"I didn't lie."

Mrs. Norman looks at me like I'm a piece of chewing gum stuck to the sole of her flip-flop that she's wearing on the best holiday ever—that I've just ruined by attaching myself to her.

"Do the right thing. Else you will regret it. And this—" She indicates the space between us. "You don't mention anything about *this* conversation. Because this isn't happening, is it? This *never* happened. This is just you, imagining things again. Got it? Good. This is our secret. You'll be seeing more of me because we've got to sort this out. And you are going to do what's right." She leans forward even more. "You'll pay if you don't."

Lies

THIS CAN'T BE REAL. AGAIN. THIS IS TOO MUCH.

IT'S NOT REAL.

I'M NOT REAL.

NOT REAL. NONE OF THIS.

IT'S JUST A STORY.

IMAGINATION.

IT'S A LIE.

I LIE. I ALWAYS LIE. THAT'S WHAT THEY SAY, SO THIS MUST BE A LIE. MY BRAIN, JUST BEING…WEIRD. MAKING STUFF UP. JUST LIKE THEY SAY.

DAMN IT, CHAOS. WHERE ARE YOU?

Blank

WHAT THE FUCK IS CHAOS DOING? THE ONLY true friend I've got, and she's gone.

Gone…

GONE.

I stab the felt-tip into my arm, picture all the insects in my blood swarming below around its point, like koi feasting on fish flakes. My ink gives my blood-insects life.

GONE. GONE. GONE.

I don't know what else to write.

I don't go to Group.

I tell them I'm not feeling well.

I stay in my room. Ella's not back. She'll have woken up at eight o'clock screaming. I wonder what the men do to her when they take her away each time. I wonder if it's like what Mr. Norman did to me. Should I ask her about it?

No. They say talking helps—but it didn't help me. Still doesn't.

I pick up *Fahrenheit 451*, but the words do little to help me. I try *Brave New World*. Then *Nineteen Eighty-Four*, but I can't concentrate, the words just blur in front of my eyes and become nothingness.

Jase knocks on my door during free-time.

"Are you coming to the attic?"

I shake my head, don't want to go upstairs to our common room. I stare at the brand on his forehead. It looks bigger than usual. Then I become aware of mine. It *is* bigger than usual.

Then I see the look on Jase's face when he sees the new words on my body. The words that appeared after I escaped from Mrs. Norman. I don't even remember doing them. Don't remember the feel of the pen in my hand.

I shut my door before he can say anything, even though we're not supposed to shut the doors in the day, and I wait for Chaos to rise. To speak, to reassure me. To tell me what the fuck I'm supposed to do with the hidden knife. Why the hell hasn't any of the staff seen it on the tapings? All that bloody CCTV.

But Chaos doesn't come.

I grit my teeth tighter and tighter, read some more until my gums throb.

It's her turn to take over. I've been awake, been *me*, for too long.

But she wasn't just sleeping, was she?

Chaos has gone.

I'm alone.

The Doctor

A DOCTOR COMES A LITTLE WHILE LATER. I don't know how long it's been. The guards stand and watch as I'm examined. He says I've got a slight fever. That's why I'm 'not myself.' The guards nod.

They give me more medication and leave.

I try to sleep.

I can't sleep. I write *FEVER* over and over across my thumb. My body is a furnace inside, and I see it. Burning coals in my bones. Is that why Chaos has gone? She's been burnt away? My body is fighting her, evicting her?

My head pounds.

No. No! I don't want her to go!

I didn't kick her out!

COME BACK, I write across my chest, pulling my T-shirt and jumper down so I can get to my skin. I write it over the other words there: BAD, INADEQUATE, UNFAVORING, GRIM, WRONG, STOP IT ALL NOW.

But my words don't summon Chaos. Panic starts to rise in me.

I can't do this on my own.

COME BACK COME BACK COME BACK. I trace over the letters, over and over and over and over, until my vision's blurring and I feel sick.

Ella returns and watches me with big puppy-dog eyes as I'm going over the K of 'back' for the seventy-first time. She sits on her bed, one leg folded underneath her.

"Are you all right?" she asks, sucking her thumb, big Disney doe-eyes on me.

I tell her I'm fine, even though I'm not. My words aren't enough. Chaos has left me.

"Are you coming to dinner?"

I tell her I'm not.

She looks worried and then leaves. I picture her going to Matt's office and reporting me to him, telling him I'm not eating. She'll stare at the photo of Justin Timberlake and her eyes will go glassy as she speaks.

I wait for five minutes before I shut the door, even though it's not nighttime. Another rule I'm breaking. But I close it and I take out the knife. Maria's knife.

I stare at the sharp blade for a long, long time. Maybe my felt-tip can't reach inside me now. Maybe Chaos is trapped deep in my burning caves and my pen can't reach her, can't stir her. Can't save her from the infernal.

But maybe the knife could.

Gently, I run the fleshy pad of my thumb over it, but I don't press down on it.

Not yet.

I'll know when I need to do something.

That's what Mum said. One of the things I clearly remember.

We were sitting at the lunch table, half-eaten tuna sandwiches on our plates. I was fussing about whether I wanted to audition for the play that year or the next.

"When the timing's right, you'll know," Mum said. "If you're doubting it now, it means next year will be better."

I stare at the thin edge of the knife, and I see all the worlds inside it. Trapped girls screaming and crying. I wonder if one of them is Chaos.

But none of them sees me.

None of them gives me the signal.

So, I put the knife away.

Proof

I HEAD TO RECEPTION. I NEED TO TELL someone about Mrs. Norman, and I need proof. They know I lie as it is. But there's a visitors' book at reception. I just need to find her name and tell them. They'll have to believe me.

Maggie's at the desk. She's pregnant. Seeing her always makes me feel strange. It does with any pregnant woman, like it's…too much. I look at her and inside her stomach I see the baby. See it as a tiny skeleton with flesh on it.

"Are you okay, dear?" Maggie looks down her nose at me.

I nod.

LIAR flashes hot on my back.

"Matt wants the visitors' book," I say, but the lie doesn't really make me feel that bad. Everyone knows I'm a liar anyway; they know I'm Untrustworthy, and lying is written into my DNA.

Maggie hands me the book, just like that.

I scamper off with it. Easy peasy.

I hug the book to my chest, put it under my jumper, and then reach the toilets. A guard stands outside, and she follows me in and tells me she'll be waiting. By that, she means listening and timing. I expect her to search me, but she doesn't. I shut the door and sit on the closed toilet lid. I wish I could lock the door, but the lock's been removed. As quietly as I can, I slide the book out from under my jumper and look through the pages. The pungent smell of disinfectant wraps around my nostrils.

I turn page after page, my eyes starting to blur with the effort.

But there's no mention. No mention of Elaine Norman or anyone visiting me. No mention at all. I peruse the logs again, certain I must've missed the page.

But there's nothing.

I look down at my hand.

IS ANY OF THIS REAL?

I jump as I see the words. The words printed on the back of my right hand in a scrawl that isn't mine. The lettering is long and thin, and slightly at a backward angle.

It's her handwriting. Chaos's.

When did she write this? I haven't been absent...

I turn my hand over.

ONLY ONE THING IS REAL. IT'S NOT SAFE HERE.

Not safe. Not safe. Not safe.

"You okay in there?" the guard calls out.

I startle and stand up quickly, nearly drop the book.

"Yes," I shout back. Then I hide the book and flush the toilet. "Coming out now."

I need to get out.

It's this place, the pills they're giving me. It has to be. The Facility somehow knows about Chaos, and everyone here is blocking her from me, disrupting our connection. It has to be this place.

What Are You Waiting For?

JASE CALLS BY MY ROOM DURING FREE-TIME again the next day. He's careful not to step over the threshold, because that's forbidden and if a camera monitor saw a guy in a girl's room, Jase would be punished severely. Sexual relations are forbidden. I don't know how Maria and Gaz have got away with it for so long.

Or maybe that's another thing I've imagined? I want to scream and keep screaming.

"Are you okay?" Jase asks. He's wearing his lace-up shoes today, but minus the laces, of course, so with every shift of his weight, his heels slip out of the backs of his trainers.

I nod.

"You not coming to the attic?"

I shake my head and stay sitting on my bed. I wish I could shut the door.

"Oh, come on. We're going to play Snakes and Ladders. The electronic set is in there now."

They regularly do that, the guards, move different games in there for us to play with like we're little children.

I press my hands more firmly into my duvet, so I can hear it laugh in its crinkly voice. "I don't want to."

"But we're doing two teams, and I can't be on my own against Maria and Gaz. You know what they're like."

Jase pleads with his eyes, and I give in. I always do when he pleads with his eyes.

As I walk to the attic with Jase, I notice Carla, one of the guards, watching us. She smiles and I'm sure she shares a hidden look with Jase. My eyes widen. That look—they've been talking about me. Talking behind my back. Talking about me…planning stuff… And Mrs. Norman, she's involved…they let her in.

My hands shake.

I look down at them. My left hand.

TRUST NO ONE, Chaos has written.

I tell Jase I forgot my notebook, and I run back to my room before he can speak.

This Doesn't Feel Right

I write the words over and over again in my notebook, trying to write them in the long, thin, angled font. Trying to make my hand do it. Because it must've been me. Those words. Or I really am going mad. And it can't have been Chaos because she doesn't like me writing on myself, and she's not been here.

Why hasn't she been here?

Oh God. She really has left me.

It was lies. All of that about needing a long rest to help me escape—it was lies! I drag in a shaking breath and look around my room. Mickey Mouse grins back at me a hundred times over from Ella's bed.

I stand up. Chaos has gone. The only person on my side has gone. Left me.

It's too hot in here.

I feel sick. My skin is clammy, and I'm sweating so much. Sweating cold sweat that stinks.

Get out.

Need to get out.

Have to—

Have to go now.

I run for the doorway, then double back.

The knife.

I need the knife.

I lift my mattress and pull it out. It gleams magnificently and tells me everything will be all right.

I run down the hall.

A figure comes into view.

It's Matt.

He sees me holding the knife. His face goes white. Then he presses a button on his radio.

I Am on Fire

A PADDED ROOM.

What the hell are you doing?

"Where have you been?" I spin around, trying to see her.

I told you to keep calm, make them think you're better. You're making this difficult!

"But you left me!" I scream, and I scream the words so loudly that the words grow and grow, and I'm in a little cell and the words are now pressing up against me, trying to suffocate me. And I can't think—everything's just a blur. A total blur that I can't make sense of.

Can't work it out.

Matt saw me with the knife. He had his radio…and then…then I was here.

I'm still here, cowering in the corner of the cell.

I'll sort this, Chaos says, her tone kinder this time. *Don't worry. You'll be out in no time. We'll be safe out there.*

THE DIARY OF BROOKE TAYLOR

Sunday, January 13th, 2013

Chaos says I should keep this record. That the police might need it. A timeline. She says to write everything down, and even though I told her I'm not going to the police because I need to keep my family safe, I'm still doing it.

I'm still writing this.

And she's told me to write this down for years. Since I was fourteen. But it's taken me nearly two years to feel I can write it. Because writing it sets it into stone. Words have a sense of permanence when written. They have form.

So my name is Brooke Taylor. I turned sixteen two weeks ago, on January 2nd. And I've been being abused by a teacher at my school called Barry Norman.

He took me to his house again on Friday. He's been doing it once or twice a week mostly for the last two years. But now it's different, because I won't be able to hide this secret. It's going to be ballooning from me.

I don't want to write what happened, because if you're reading this then I've probably taken this to the police and you already know. This is just to show the dates or something. And you're going to think I'm mad because I'm the only one who hears Chaos.

But I'm not mad.

I'm lonely.

I'm a victim.

And Chaos is the only one who's been helping me. She only helps people who need help.

But it's not enough.

Please can you help me?

Tuesday, January 29th, 2013

Again today, and also a few days ago. I was too upset to write. Sometimes it's worse than others.

Saturday, February 23rd, 2013

I'm not good at writing this regularly, but there's a CCTV camera on his neighbor's house. I think it covers Barry Norman's side-door. The one he always takes me through. You can get the records off his neighbor if you need to, can't you? See how often it's happening, match some of the dates to this.

Wednesday, February 27th, 2013

I tried to run away today, during it. I got outside. But he caught me.

Saturday, March 9th, 2013

It happened again, yesterday. At his house. But I'm going mad. I thought I heard another girl there. A girl crying.

I don't understand. He told me I was special. Just me.

Tuesday, March 12th, 2013

It hasn't happened again, but I can't stop thinking about that other girl I heard last Friday. She was real. I'm sure of it. Chaos thinks so, too, says there's a basement and that's where the other girl is.

I've been trying to work out who she is. The last few days at school, I've been watching his office when I can. Trying to see if any other girls are going in there.

Fiona changed schools. It can't be her.

I know he used to give Raven a lot of detentions too, but Raven's barely in any more. I wonder if he's left too.

And it was definitely a girl.

Friday, March 15th, 2013

At Barry Norman's house, it was just silent today. No girl crying. Maybe the cries I heard last week were mine?

I asked him if he had a basement. He just laughed.

But he can't have a basement, can he? Else he'd have taken me there.

And I'm not there.

He always takes me to the master bedroom.

Wednesday, April 24th, 2013

Oh God. I can't even write this. But I can't ignore the… thing.

Inside me.

It moved today.

And I don't know what to do.

Wednesday, May 15th, 2013

I haven't written much because I don't like going over it. And it's always the same.

Except for one difference today: Mr. Norman has a black eye. In class, he said he'd walked into a door handle. But door handles aren't at eye level.

It's made me wonder about other girls again. Whether it's not just me.

Monday, June 24th, 2013

Exams at school today. I messed up. Barry Norman was proctoring. I felt too sick to concentrate. On my way, he told me to come back to his room to discuss the paper.

I didn't go back.

Raven was watching me from the school gates. I didn't go back because he was watching. And I don't know why or what it means.

Friday, July 12th, 2013

Mum and Dad finally noticed. I knew it was coming, knew there was only so long clothes would cover up what he's done to me. Surprising it's taken this long, actually.

They're angry.

But I can't tell them.

We're not speaking.

And they just can't SEE.

Thursday, August 1st, 2013

He found me in the post office. The last two years, the summer holidays have been a break away from him. Not this time. He wanted to congratulate me.

Monday, August 19th, 2013

He was angrier today.

Wednesday, August 21st, 2013

Still really angry.

And I saw a pack of sanitary towels on his kitchen counter. I don't understand. Mrs. Norman is in the process of divorcing him, I think. All her clothes and books and makeup disappeared a while ago.

Thursday, August 29th, 2013

There's a house on the same lane as Barry Norman's for sale. I saw it in the estate agent's window. Four bedrooms. Two reception rooms. A basement that's been turned into a gym.

A basement.

Monday, September 2nd, 2013

I need to get inside the basement. I can't stop thinking about it.

But I can't make him suspicious of me.

Wednesday, September 4th, 2013

First day back at school. Can't believe my parents are making me go. It was terrible—exactly as predicted. Everyone was pointing at me, whispering, making nasty comments.

And he just kept smiling at me. First time I've seen him in a few weeks, and all he did was smile. No detentions. Nothing.

Saturday, September 14th, 2013

Couldn't write yesterday, didn't feel well after it all. I thought maybe he wouldn't want me anymore—now I look like this—but it appears it's back on.

He's had a haircut. Looks stupid.

No luck searching the house. Couldn't find a basement. And it was so quiet. If there was a girl in there, she'd make noise, wouldn't she? She'd hear me?

But she'd hear his voice too.

Or maybe she's gagged.

Chaos says I need to report this.

Tuesday, October 1st, 2013

The thing is here.

Saturday, November 2nd, 2013

I lost my diary for the last month. I don't understand how it went missing when I'm always so careful to put it under the foot-end of my mattress. And it's not like I'm even at school now. One day it was there, then it wasn't.

Today I found it back there.

Weird.

The lock was still on it.

No one can have read it.

The last two weeks have been pretty much the 'usual'— for what that means now. Because everything's changed. It should be easier. I'm too busy to go to his house. But he's too clever and he offers extra tuition and says to my parents he can get me back in school sooner than they all thought. So of course they take him up on his extra lessons and it doesn't matter how loudly I scream.

And I think there is a girl or woman there, hidden somewhere. An extra toothbrush has appeared in the bathroom. Just a toothbrush—no clothes, nothing else. Mr. Norman didn't like me commenting on the toothbrush.

Thursday, November 28th, 2013

I've got to do something.

TUESDAY, FEBRUARY 4TH, 2014
EIGHT WEEKS AFTER MISS
TAYLOR'S ADMISSION TO THE
DE HEWITT FACILITY

UNIVERSITY OF EXETER

Name: Emilia Johnson

Age: 19

Birthday: September 14, 1994

Place of birth: Swansea

Card Number: 072562548 Expiry Date: 18/06/2018

The Outside World

I AM OUT. OUT OF THE FACILITY. I TAKE IN THE fresh air and struggle to get used to my body again. I've never been away from it for so long. But Chaos has filled me in: the program healed me, and the guards were pleased. They let me out. We didn't even have to escape.

I stare at my forehead in a shop window's reflection. There's no branding, even though the 'O' should have been replaced with an 'H'. I should have 'UH' on my forehead, but they removed it all. I wonder if the process was painful. I squint, trying to see the marks left behind. Because there always must be marks. Something as bad as that cannot be removed without a trace. You can't erase history, pretend these things didn't happen.

But I can't see any marks at all.

It's my eyes, my vision, bad. Has to be.

I open my rucksack and see some of the items: half-empty bottle of wine, a woolly hat, and Maria's knife. I balk a little. How did Chaos manage to keep this? I pull out the hat, put it on so it covers my forehead—just in case. Because the marks, the impressions left behind, they have to be there, right?

I am in Exeter, in Devon, England—I don't know how I know, but I just do—and I have a new identity now. I can't be Kira Taylor anymore, because people are looking for her. Bad people who will want me dead because of what I did. Because of the murder. So I am Emilia Johnson now. For someone who's been cured of her Untrustworthy nature, my whole life will now be a lie.

But it's a good lie. One that will keep me safe.

And I couldn't stay at The Facility. Not when Mrs. Norman knew where I was.

Chaos must have told them this, because the guards at The Facility have set up a whole new life for me.

I'm at the bus station, and I'm a university student, in this new life. I'm doing an English degree—the welcome pack is in my bag. Chaos told me that my support worker at The

Facility said she thought I'd like it, that it has some creative writing modules I can opt into. She thought it would help strengthen my voice.

For a moment, it feels like the world's closing in as I stare around me. The moody, gray sky is pushing down on me, and the earth is pushing up. The air is too thick, filled with smoke and raindrops and tangy smells and shouts from the people around me.

And the people! There are so many. Men in suits walking quickly. Women who look tired. Other women who are dressed immaculately and carefully carry handbags. Other teenagers—around my age or maybe a little younger—who gaggle together, talking about music and the rain and "that awful person."

I flinch and look at them. My breaths come out too sharp.

I look down at my hands.

Clean. They scrubbed me. On The Facility's mini-bus—that's what Chaos told me. I push my sleeves up, stare at every new inch of bare skin that I discover. My words, gone.

"Watch it, love!" a man suddenly says, and then he's patting me on the back, and I turn, dazed, and—

A seagull flies at me.

I duck.

A bus starts up ten feet from me, honking its horn.

A woman runs toward it.

Someone drops their disposable coffee cup, and it rolls across the concrete.

I jump back, just as the cup is about to hit my shoe—

I'm wearing high heels.

I stumble, partly in shock, partly in some sort of strange realization that I can walk in them. When I know I shouldn't be able to. I've never been able to.

I catch sight of myself in the plastic division between the bus platform and the seating area. My hair is black. Dyed. I'm wearing makeup. Thick, dark black lines around my eyes.

I look down at myself then back at my reflection, taking in my clothes. Dark purple tights, a short, black leather skirt. A black hoodie. And a black backpack.

You must match the image of Emilia Johnson.

I nod. Of course.

But where do I go? I wait for Chaos to speak again. But she doesn't.

No. Of course she wouldn't. She's tired. She's done so much in the past few days.

It's just me here. Maybe she didn't even say those words just now. Maybe that was me. Or a memory of what she said, what she explained—because she said it all so fast when we swapped over. I couldn't process it all. No, of course I couldn't. I only took a certain amount in, so the rest is still sinking in. That's what that was.

So, my file. I've got a file. The fake file for Emilia Johnson. I remember that. Where is it?

I look down at my hands—was I holding it before? Holding it against my chest…like it could shield me… But there's just thin air now. I adjust my woolly hat, suddenly self-conscious. All these people around me know what to do—they're queuing up and getting on buses and talking to each other and everything's okay for them. Isn't it? I used to know what to do, even when I was branded with just the U.

But now that's gone. My identity, lost.

LOST.

The word should be on my right thigh. It *should* be there. It's part of me. But I know it's gone. My fingers burn. I look around, hear a strange rushing sound in my ears. I gulp. My throat feels strange. Raw.

RAW.

I look to the long wooden bench at the back of the platform, and I see a man sitting there with a damp newspaper and a dripping umbrella. A girl is beside him, earphones in. Two old ladies are next with canvas bags full of shopping. And a woman tapping a beautiful Bic against a notebook.

My eyes light up—that's the only way to describe what it feels like.

I need it, the pen.

I need it.

And then I'm walking over to her.

I point at the pen, feel words trying to escape, but I hold them back, like I hold everything back and—

"Can I help you?" Her voice is loud, abrasive. It cuts me. Cuts words into me.

I'm leaning right over her.

Shit.

I step back and—

"Watch it!"

Scalding liquid splashes over me. I cry out, and then there's another woman in front of me, and she's asking if I'm okay, if it burnt me. I stare at them.

Get out. Get out. Get out.

The woman with the pen and notebook is standing up now, looking at me strangely.

I grab her pen, and I run.

Two Beady Eyes

I AM IN A ROOM WITH A RAT AND TWO bottles of gin.

I freeze, eyes wide, stare at the creature. What the hell?

How did I?

I was running and—

Just listen, Chaos snarls. *I was in no fucking state to control you again, but look, you were just going to mess this up. I had to take over. We don't want you drawing attention to yourself.*

So, update: here's what you did under my command…step by step.

You got your phone out because the address of your new house was on it, just like I already told you. You launched Google Maps, typed in Pennsylvania Road, and you walked to your house just as the rain worsened and the wind kicked in.

You walked up to the door. I made you hesitate a little as I know how bloody nervous you are all the time and we've got to be consistent. God, can you tell I'm angry and sleep-deprived?

You knocked on the door.

The door creaked open. A gangly teenager stood there. You didn't know why you thought of him as a gangly teenager—or why I did—but we both did. Do.

"You Emilia?" The gangly teenager looked you up and down.

You nodded.

Again, he looked you up and down.

"I've come for the room." I had to prompt you then, to speak.

Another look up and down. "Rob said you were coming." He grunted. "Just make sure you pay on time. Rent goes to Beth as it all comes out of her account. But pay her the night before it's due—she'll give you her bank details. No smoking in the house. If you buy drink, expect Cassie to drink it before you even get it in the house. You checked in with Steve—the landlord?"

"Yes," you said. And then you listened to him explain all the arrangements that have been made—but really, you don't need to know any of that. Not when you don't even listen and just panic anyway.

The gangly teenager let you in. The house smelled of sweat, too much deodorant, and alcohol. The lanky teenager showed you up to a room on the second floor.

"Yours."

You opened the door, and we did a double take.

"There's a rat in there."

"And that's a problem?" The guy had a smarmy look on his face that made me want to cuss loudly. I almost felt sorry for you here, you having to live with him. Us both having to live with him.

"It's a rat."

"It's a boy. He's Freddie. He comes with the room."

"He comes with the room?"

"If you don't like him, just let him go in the woods or something." He snorted. "Thought all girls liked pets."

"I don't like disease-ridden ones."

"That's prejudiced thinking. And people like you are the reasons rats get a bad name."

He stalked off and you were left looking at my room, and the rat in it.

You tried to ignore the rat as you looked about. A bed. A wardrobe. A desk—with the rat's cage on it. Freddie. He looked at you expectantly, and I wondered if he could see me inside.

We turned our back on him. This was the point where you'd normally reach for a pen and carve all sorts of bad words on your skin. But I was in charge of you—so you didn't.

You unpacked your things like a good little girl. A phone, lots of documentation to do with your new course. Passwords for online portals and reading lists and transcriptions of Emilia's past exam results. A timetable too—your first seminar is tomorrow. Fun times. (You need to read Pride and Prejudice for it. The eBook is on your phone.)

Then you put your clothes in the wardrobe. You don't have many, but we'll go shopping tomorrow after the seminar. Hopefully you can be in control then, and I can just watch.

Okay, got it?

Now, you're all right, Kira—don't start panicking now. You're about to go down and eat dinner with your new housemates. Okay? Good.

Now, you're in charge.

Don't mess this up.

If we go back to The De Hewitt Facility, Elaine Norman will get us.

What Kind of Game is This?

DINNER? WITH MY NEW HOUSEMATES?

The roof of my mouth dries. No. Why would she do that—Chaos? She knows I can't eat when it's daylight and—

Oh God.

I take a deep breath. Look around my room.

The rat watches me. My pet rat?

This is… This is just…

My hands ache to write my words.

I sit on the bed and stare at my lap, at the super-short skirt. It's still wet from the rain. All my clothes are.

This is me now.

I take a deep breath.

See the pen on the desk. It's on top of the stack of papers.

I lunge for it, relish the way it fits into my hand.

Then I push back the sleeves of the sodden black hoodie. I stare at my skin: so clean, the perfect parchment. No words at all.

I start filling in my words again.

ALONE. HELP. SCARED. TOMATO.

I don't know where that last one comes from. It wasn't there before. But it appears on my right arm, like it belongs here. And it does. It is its home now. Everyone needs a home.

The pen itches for more words to be released, and so I have to listen, obey.

LISTEN. FEAR. QUIET. HURT. JASE. JASE. JASE.

Jase?

When the pen is finished, I roll my sleeves back down and check the words are hidden. I don't know why it's important now—it's never been important before—but it is now. And they're hidden. I almost look ordinary.

Ordinary is good. Need to hide.

Have to hide.

There's a knock on the door.

I freeze.

The knock comes again.

Then: "Emilia?"

I open the door, feel strange, like a robot. A robot who just does stuff—stuff without meaning to, stuff without even concentrating.

The girl standing in the doorway is beautiful. A model. Blond hair that's tousled, like she's just stepped off a runway or out of a salon. Immediately, I feel inferior with my scruffy, graffitied body.

I want to run and hide.

Hide. Hide. Hide.

A fizzing sensation fills my fingertips.

"I'm Cassie," the girl says.

"Cassie," I say. Automatically, I reach for my hat, pull it down a little. What if it was too high up, the edge? What if she sees the redness that has to be there by now and realizes I've had a branding removed and—

Oh, God. I'm breathing too quickly. She's looking at me strangely. No. No. No.

"Uh, we're going to eat as a house," Cassie says. And she's still got that look in her eyes, the look I know—the one that means she's assessing me.

I've got to do better than this. Got to. Got to. Got to.

"So, you coming down?"

I nod quickly. Too quickly. But need to be normal.

Cassie smiles. "We're not as scary as we look. Well, Rob is. But I'm sure he'll like you. Same taste in music." She gestures at me, and I suddenly realize I'm not wearing the black hoodie anymore, and the world can see the shirt I'm wearing. Black, with long sleeves that I must've pushed up before, along with the hoodie's sleeves. This shirt has a *Death Becomes* logo.

Death Becomes? I don't even know what that is. But it's got long sleeves. My words are hidden. That's good.

"Words are precious," I mutter, then flinch when I realize I've said it out loud. Shit. Shit. Shit. Way to act normal, Kira. No, *Emilia*.

Cassie stares at me, probably trying to work out what the hell is wrong with me. And what is wrong with me?

Nervous. Just nervous.

And she's waiting for an answer, isn't she?

I hear the rat moving in his cage behind me, and I feel like I'm part of a video game, waiting for my player to decide what to do—and why is she taking so long? There are only three options—easy to choose.

1) LAUGH AND SAY OF COURSE AND FOLLOW CASSIE DOWNSTAIRS AND MEET

EVERYONE AND START YOUR NORMAL
LIFE.

2) TELL CASSIE YOU CAN'T SPEAK
BUT GO ANYWAY. [BUT HOW DO I TELL
HER? SEE OPTION 3]

3) GRAB A PIECE OF PAPER AND WRITE
THAT YOU HAVE AN INJURED VOICE BOX
AND CANNOT SPEAK AT THE MOMENT, BUT
YOU'LL COME AND MEET EVERYONE.

Only I've spoken to her, already—so two and three won't work—and the only other option is one. And all of them end with me meeting everyone.

What kind of game is this?

"Yes," I say.

And then I'm following Cassie downstairs. But this isn't real. It can't be…can't be.

As I walk, I think about the list of options that just appeared in my head. The video game options. Choose your own adventure.

I like adventures.

And I like lists, because I like writing lists, like feeling in control and organized.

So I make another one, and my fingers write it against my thigh as I climb down the stairs. My to-do list:

1) MEET EVERYONE.
2) FEED THE RAT.
3) DON'T FEED YOURSELF.
4) READ PRIDE AND PREJUDICE.

Blend In

THEY'RE ALL EATING CHICKEN TIKKA MASALA, pilau rice, garlic bread, and mango chutney, and drinking beers, when Cassie and I get to the living room. The other housemates. *My* other housemates, lounging on a sofa that looks a little too worn and blue beanbags with dark stains on.

Cassie introduces them.

The lanky teenager is Bradley.

The boy in the *Death Becomes* hoodie is Rob.

The other girl is Beth. She likes rice. I watch as she devours two portions, mixing it with the gloopy mango chutney.

Bradley tells me that Beth has had a bad day. Her boyfriend has been a dick to her.

"You should just dump him," Bradley says to her. "He treats you like shit."

"I know," Beth says, deadpan. She shoves more rice and chutney into her mouth. Her lipstick is smeared. So is her eye makeup.

I stir my wooden fork in my bowl of curry, then flinch. I've got curry, too. When did that happen? What the hell? I stare at it on my lap, stare at my legs on the sofa. I'm sitting down. Have I eaten any?

I touch my lips, don't think I have… I try to smell my breath, but it's suddenly too hot in the room. My eyes smart.

"You all right?" Rob's looking at me strangely. It's the first time I've heard his voice. I don't like his voice.

I jump up, pushing the bowl of curry onto the coffee table. It clanks against beer bottles, and the chink of it sends chills down my spine.

"Water!" I manage, and then I rush out.

The kitchen, I can see it.

Then I'm in it, running the tap and cupping water in my hands and drinking from it like I'm in primary school. There are glasses on the side, but I imagine all the germs on them, and each germ has a pulsing, bright green body, and a thousand hairy legs, and googly eyes that watch me.

My stomach churns. I place my hand against it.

What's happening?

Zoned out. Lost time. I've lost time.

And I've eaten—but no! I can't have! That wasn't on my list.

No…not on the agenda, the plan.

What kind of game is this?

"Not a good game, not a good game, not a good game," I mutter.

But it's *not* a game, is it?

Unless these people are players, too? Cassie and Beth and Rob and Bradley? Could they be players, players like me?

I splash water onto my face, and then turn. Look around. There's a controller on the table. A games controller. I don't know what it's for because I'm not a gamer, but…

But I don't need it.

This game.

I'm *in* it.

It's not just a horrible dystopian world I'm in.

It's a horrible dystopian video game.

And someone's controlling me.

I flinch, feel sicker than ever.

Oh God.

Chaos is in my head. Her. *She's* my handler. I'm the character. She's playing me.

I lift my hand up, spraying water everywhere. But that was my decision—not Chaos's. Mine.

I'm in control.

I'm in the game.

And the goal?

Every game has a goal. There has to be a goal in a game, otherwise it's a rubbish game.

And then the words flash in front of me, written in bright neon letters that flash and flash and flash and make me dizzy.

GOAL: BLEND IN AND REMAIN HIDDEN SO THE MONSTER CAN'T FIND YOU.

The monster. Barry Norman. He's the monster.

"Blend in," I say. "Remain hidden."

I turn quickly. A pen. I need a pen. Need to write it down.

Goals must be written down. Have to be.

I search the cluttered kitchen table, distilling papers and dirty cutlery and mugs with soggy teabags still in them. And a Monopoly box.

I stare at it. A game within a game. My eyes narrow. What does that mean? What is its significance? It must have significance…it must.

Roaring sounds fill my ears.

"You all right? Shit, Emilia!"

I jump, turn, find Rob rushing into the kitchen, going for the sink. The overflowing sink. He turns the tap off. The roar disappears. He plunges his hand into the full sink, pulls the plug out.

"Sorry," I squeak. Squeak. Like the rat.

The rat.

He's part of the game.

The rat. What's the significance of a rat in a video game? I don't know, and I need to find it out. I put it at the top of my to-do list.

"You nearly flooded the kitchen!" Rob shouts, and he shouts the words so loudly, and I shrink back, heart pounding.

"Sorry!"

"Hey!" Cassie appears. "What's going on?"

"Sorry—left the tap on… I'm just tired. Been up for so long. I'll go and take a rest," I say, and I run. Run as fast as I can.

My stomach tightens, and my heart gets even faster the closer I am to my bedroom door—my safe zone, my place to recharge, my place to get new lives. Replenish. I shut the door, and grab a pen. The beautiful Bic from the woman in the bus station.

REPLENISH. NEW LIFE. STAY HIDDEN. THEY MUSTN'T FIND ME.

As soon as the words are out of my system, a weight lifts from my shoulders, like I'm not being pushed down into the carpet anymore.

An extra life—it has to be. Yes. This is what it is.

I nod slowly, turn and—

And I see the window. It's fogged up with condensation, and it's dark outside, but I see the words on it. The words written on the foggy pane with a finger.

YOU ARE NOT ALONE.

I scream.

Things That Chaos Told Me

"YOU ARE NOT ALONE," MR. NORMAN SAID AS he stroked the side of Brooke's neck with his thick calloused hands. "You're never alone, Brooke. You've got me now."

In the full-length mirror, Brooke saw his pupils dilate. He was standing behind her, holding her against his body. Their eyes met in the reflection, and he smiled.

"I care very much about you." His voice was darker than before, slightly more primitive. "You know that, don't you? You'll never be alone now."

Brooke shouldn't have told him about how alone she felt as an Untrustworthy, how all her friends had dumped her the moment the Detector Room gave that result. But she did tell him, in a moment of weakness on maybe the fifth or the sixth time he brought her back here. To his house. In this room with the full-length mirror that captures what they do. He asked what she was thinking. Brooke told him she was thinking of her old friends and how alone she was now. He didn't like that, and since then he's always told her that she's not alone. Maybe she was trying to appeal to him? I don't know—and neither does Chaos. We've puzzled over this for a while.

At some point, it changed. Brooke changed. She just…accepted him. Accepted what he was doing, though eventually she would write it all in her diary. But accepting it, then, in that very small way, made her feel special. Made her feel lucky. Made her feel beautiful in the only way an Untrustworthy can feel beautiful.

Beautiful for someone else.

Not her.

He touched Brooke's sternum gently, jolting her out of her thoughts.

"I'll always be here, always be watching you. Come on." He led her toward the bed, and Brooke's reflection begged her to do something. It screamed silently at her to run.

But she didn't.

She knew how fast he could chase.

The Next Player in This Horrible Dystopian Game

THE DOOR OF EMILIA'S BEDROOM FLIES OPEN, and Cassie and Bradley rush in.

I'm still screaming, but I stop when I see them.

"What is it?"

They stare at me.

I stare at them.

I'm shaking.

I point at the window.

But—but the words have gone.

Gone.

Just like your sanity.

I flinch, don't know where that voice came from. Because it wasn't Chaos—not my voice, my handler, the person controlling me, the character and—

It *wasn't* her. Another voice.

Another player?

Or a commentator? Do video games have commentaries? Or narrations?

Yes, a narrator.

"*Emilia?*"

They're staring at me, Cassie and Bradley.

I let out another squeak, like the rat's. Hold on, do rats even squeak?

Tears pierce the corners of my eyes.

I don't know.

I don't know whether rats squeak.

"Was it the spider?" Cassie asks.

"Spider?" My eyes widen. A spider and a rat. What noise does a spider make?

Cassie marches past me, then goes to my wardrobe. It's next to the window. The window with the condensation on. The condensation that's a smooth, fuzzy blanket. No words.

No words.

"Yeah, it's a big-ass spider," Cassie says, now bending down and looking behind the wardrobe. The side of her face smushes into the wall.

I wait for the wall to swallow her.

It doesn't.

It's a nice wall.

"God," Bradley says. "Girls and spiders. Didn't need to scream the whole place down, did you?"

"Sorry," I say, and I keep saying the word over and over in my head, until they leave.

Until it's just me and the rat, and I don't know what he means, why he's here, what his purpose is. To help me hide from the monster? Or to expose me? To tell everyone who I am. To leave clues for the monster to find me?

I'm jittery as I change into the single pair of pajamas that I own. Or that Emilia owns. But that's me now.

Me.

I lie in bed, listen to the howling wind and rain outside.

My stomach rumbles.

I'm hungry.

I wait for Monika to bring me food.

But she doesn't.

Her player isn't clever. Hasn't found a way to track my character, to find me here.

Even if The Facility did arrange for me to come here…
But this house isn't in a Lowers' block. Is it? And it should be, shouldn't it? I should only be with other Lowers. That's right, isn't it? Only I can't think. Can't quite remember. There's a fog all around me, like I've climbed inside that windowpane now.

Because I'm hiding in a new place.

A safe new place.

A place where I'm not alone.

Disguise

THERE'S A MIRROR IN THE BATHROOM ON THE
second floor. It's next to my room, and I lock myself in there
early the next morning with my pen and gulp down the rest
of one of the bottles of gin that was next to the rat's cage.
Don't know when I opened it, but most of it was gone when
I woke up. Must've had it last night.

I put my pen on the glass shelf above the sink, place the
empty gin bottle next to it, and then I strip my pajamas off.

I stare at myself. Even with the words I hastily scribbled
last night—*ALONE, HELP, SCARED, TOMATO, LISTEN, FEAR,
QUIET, HURT, JASE, JASE, JASE*—my body looks like an alien.
My ribs are like pencils in a case. My forehead has the
imprint of wool across it—I slept with my hat on—and in

the too-bright, yellow light I can't really see the redness from the letter removal. I risk a smile, then decide I look better smiling without teeth. As if my teeth will give me away. They've always been a bit too crooked, and you can't disguise teeth; at my old dentist surgery there was a poster up saying that everyone's set of teeth is unique to them. No two people have the same teeth, and I remember wondering if that applied to identical twins too—even though Brooke and I weren't identical—only I never asked, and now suddenly I wish I had. Knowledge is power. And there are people who want to hurt me.

I turn and twist so I can see my spine in the mirror. The way its little nodules try and push through my skin, like it's the armor of an alien trying to escape. Because nothing wants to be trapped inside me.

You said it, girl.

I pick up my pen, and I start writing. I keep to the places I can cover though, giving my words more friends. Mustn't draw attention to myself.

I start with the familiar words. ALONE, HELP, BAD, LIAR, MIRROR.

But then the writing changes. It becomes Chaos's handwriting, and I'm writing direct-address sentences across my thighs. She's talking, and I'm the only one who can listen. The only one the words are meant for. So I reply and promise never to let another person know about this conversation.

We talk on and on, to myself, on myself, like this, and in the back of my head—somewhere, far away—there's a voice screaming at me that this isn't normal. That I'm not normal. That Mr. Norman was right.

Maybe Chaos is sick of being trapped inside me.

I set the pen down and survey myself in the full-length mirror. If I close one eye, all the words on my skin blur and become a pattern. I like it best when things blur together.

I run the water in the bath. Run it as hot as I can stand and then lie down in it, so the water covers my ears and only my eyes and nose and mouth have air. I splash about with my hands, creating waves. I know I shouldn't be able to feel the ink from my body running off, fading, swirling in the water. But I can.

And now my words are on the water's surface. As I pull the plug, my words are excited, spiraling down the drain, through pipes and into systems. They'll reach the sea, maybe, and the words will be free then. They'll swim away, and they'll grow up to be beautiful dolphins who'll later get caught again—because no one's free in this world, not really.

Even now, their shadows are left on me. Some of the words are still readable if I look carefully, inside myself. The words that I wrote the biggest. *BAD. LIAR. HELP.* They're still here, imprinted on the underside of my skin, bleeding murkiness through to the outside world, like a pen pushing through velvet. Others—like the direct-address passages and the replies written on my thighs—have blurred.

Yes. Good. I smile.

I brought no towel, and I can only use black towels that don't betray the ink. There are white towels in here. And a pink Disney princess one that I think must be Cassie's.

I shake myself dry and stand here until I'm cold and shivering. Then I pull on the pajamas I was wearing all night and clean the bath. Get rid of any lingering ink.

Ink is wonderful. I've often thought that.

Spies

ROB IS STANDING OUTSIDE THE BATHROOM when I leave. I watch him warily, but he doesn't do anything. Just watches me. I don't know why he's up here. Bradley said earlier the second floor was the girls' floor.

"He's watching you because he's a spy in the game," the rat says as I return to my room to put some proper clothes on.

I'm surprised because I didn't think rats could speak, and I stare at it.

"You need a new to-do list," the rat says.

The rat is right.

So I make a brand new one because I can't remember where the other one is or what it was I wanted to add to it.

```
1) ASK OTHERS IF THE RAT SPEAKS
TO THEM.
2) ACTUALLY DON'T.
3) FEED THE RAT.
4) WORK OUT IF THE RAT IS A SPY.
5) STAY HIDDEN [DOES THAT MEAN
BLEND IN? THIS MIGHT BE DIFFICULT
AS I'M SUPPOSED TO GO TO MY FIRST
SEMINAR TODAY.]
6) SHIT!    READ    PRIDE    AND
PREJUDICE!
```

My heart threatens to burst as I think about it all. My first seminar—and I'm not prepared. Shit. Shit. Shit.

I look around, frantic, eyes searching for a pen.

But I can't go to a seminar. I can't. The thought of going to university sends curls of heavy dread to my stomach.

School was bad enough. Those first days each September, where I'd wake—having barely slept—hours early, my stomach a rage of pain. I'd shake and shake, look like a ghost in the mirror.

Everyone says first days are always the worst. But, for me, it felt different. It was different, because of what I was. What The Detector Room marked me as.

Others would fall into their friendship circles in the playground, and they'd have seen friends in the summer holiday.

But me… I had no friends. No friendly face would greet me. I'd stand in the playground, shaking, trembling, feeling so sick. I'd walk into the buildings, through the corridors, flinching at the artificial lighting, flinching at the sounds of my peers. And they'd watch me. Their eyes would narrow.

"Bad," they'd say. "Bad. Bad. Bad."

I'd have a pen in my hand, and I'd write *BAD* on my right palm as I walked, over and over.

BAD BAD BAD.

That first day back last year was awful. The worst, all because…

I freeze. Because *what?*

My eyes narrow. There's something there—something in my memory, something trying to push forward.

It's nothing, Chaos says quickly.

Nothing?

I exhale slowly.

Just first-day nerves. Calm down, I'll tell you a story.

A Trip Down Memory Lane

(except it's not the memory lane you think it is, because I wouldn't be so cruel)

You walk back to the house that you grew up in. It's an old house. Several hundred years. Maybe even a thousand. Its previous owner swears it should've been in the Doomsday book.

In front of your house is Raven, and you're surprised because you haven't seen him in years. Not since he disappeared. Taken by the men in black who took your roommate at The Facility. Yes, this is very much a different timeline here—yes, Raven was with you at The De Hewitt Facility—no, don't even think about interrupting—for God's sake, Kira, just let me tell this damn story.

Raven seems pleased to see you, because he smiles and then you're embracing. You feel safe with him, and you hold each other close.

"Shall we go in?" you say, and you motion to the front door.

You know your parents are inside, and you want nothing more than to go and have a relaxing bath because you've been on your feet all day dealing with patients who have the flu. You're immune to flu but you know you have to look after your health. You need to go to sleep, but now Raven is here, and you also know he wants you to tell your parents.

Raven nods and whispers words into your ear, and those words make you feel warm and tingly.

You smile into each other's eyes, and you nearly get lost in them. But would it be so bad to lose yourself in Raven? You know the answer is no, and you smile.

Your parents open the door, and they smile like they already know.

"Congratulations," your mother says, and you realize they've known all the time because Raven gives you a wry grin, but you're not annoyed with him.

And then there's a party inside, and it's for the baby. Your baby. The one you are pregnant with.

Everything happens so quickly, but you go along with it because it doesn't seem odd to you. Not at all. And it's all you've ever wanted, to be part of a loving family and to be KIND and COMPASSIONATE and a DOCTOR (not just 'likely to be a doctor,' but the real thing) and now you have a baby in your arms, because time is a bit weird and slippery, and Raven is staring at you both like you're the most precious things in his world.

And you are.

Unmarked

WHEN I FORCE MYSELF TO VENTURE DOWNSTAIRS, I'm greeted by the strong smell of leftover curry and beer. I try to hold my breath as I look in the fridge. Everything in there has a Post-it note on with a name. It seems curry is the only thing Emilia's housemates share.

I'm not sure why I'm looking in the fridge, because there's no way I can eat. My stomach is so tight it's painful. I feel sick. There's a tightness in front of my eyes that makes every step seem like it's a difficult feat, difficult for me not to fall over.

The smell of the curry is making everything worse.

"Shame there's not a Freshers' Week this time of year to welcome you in."

I jump at the voice and turn to find Rob. He's wearing the same *Death Becomes* hoodie as yesterday, along with boxers and neon-orange socks. I hurriedly look away.

"Oh well. At least you ain't hung over or slept with someone you shouldn't have." He gestures to the fridge. "You ain't got any food in yet? Have some of my bread."

He stares at me, and with a jolt I realize he's looking at my forehead, and I haven't got my hat on. Immediately, I want to turn away—want to, but can't. Can't move. I feel my face redden, and I start to turn, to look for his bread in the fridge.

My heart pounds harder, faster as I reach for the pack of Hovis. I know my forehead shows nothing there now—the redness has faded. It's unmarked, unblemished. But if he knows who I am, I'll have failed the game. He'll call the monster. And the monster will kill me. I don't know how many lives I've got left.

Rob clears his throat. "What did you say your name was?"

"Emilia." I don't look at him, just busy myself with getting a slice of bread out of the bag. The loaf is too crumbly.

"Age?" Rob steps closer. He stinks.

I glance up at him.

"Eighteen." I wince as I look at him. Can I pass for an eighteen-year-old? Or was Emilia supposed to be nineteen? I can't remember.

"You're studying English, right?"

I nod.

"Me, too. I looked at your timetable yesterday. We've got the same seminar first today. Before the lecture, too. Weird. Eat that, and I'll take you there. Can show you around a bit. This campus is well different to the one in Plymouth."

Plymouth? I stare at him.

"Where you transferred from?" he says, giving me a look.

Frantically, I nod. It's suddenly very hot in the kitchen, and I'm sweating. I try to step away, but my legs won't work.

"I'll just go and get ready," Rob says. He reaches over for the bag of bread that's still in my hands, yanking it away. A small fraction of bread stays in my grip, and I watch as he dumps the rest of the slice in the toaster. "It sometimes burns one side, so keep an eye on it, and be ready to leave in twenty."

I squeeze my morsel of bread tighter and tighter between my thumb and forefinger as I watch him go.

Every part of me tells me to run, to go.

But I can't.

My stomach rumbles. I can't remember when the last time I ate was, but I can't eat the bread. I stare at it as I smell the toaster. A faint garlic smell whirls up, reminds me of when Dad put garlic bread in our toaster at home. But it's not enough to distract me, and my eyes water at the thought of putting a small piece of bread or toast in my mouth. I know how it will feel—it'll be turning stale, clogging up my mouth.

I put the scrap of bread on the counter, turn the toaster off on the wall, then pull a hand through my tangled hair before realizing I'm getting breadcrumbs there.

Escape. Escape. Escape.

Need to escape.

NEW GOAL: ESCAPE.

Just Play the Game

I DON'T ESCAPE. I WALK TO CAMPUS WITH ROB, because blending in is the main goal, and Chaos told me that the goal of escaping wasn't a real goal. It was something sent by the monster to distract me. I'm safe, if I'm on campus.

It's drizzling, though the sky threatens more rain—it rained a lot during the night—and Rob walks too close to me. I don't like it. He has the same build as Mr. Norman. Instinctively, I hug myself closer. My phone is in my pocket, and my pen in the other.

I want to reach for the pen I packed in Emilia's backpack. I want to write on the pavement. I want to write my way back to Jase and The Facility, because these new people… I don't know them, but everyone's got badness in them. At least at The Facility, people are prepared. But not here.

Never out here.

"My sister was murdered," Rob says, kicking a can along the wet tarmac. He looks at me sideways.

I gulp.

"I'm not expecting you to say anything. It's a blessing that you don't," Rob says. "I don't have to listen to your *I'm so sorry, Rob* speech where you seem to think that you need to take the blame. But she was murdered a year ago today, and sometimes I just need to talk. And you look like her, Emilia. She was called Steph. She liked the whole Goth look, too—though she did it better than you. Anyway, when I'm talking to you now, it's like I'm talking to her. And for once she can't talk back—because she was always doing that and it was *so* damn annoying. So don't say anything, okay?"

I try to walk faster, but Rob's strides are bigger than mine, and he keeps up easily.

"There are bad people out here, aren't there? People who should stay locked up." He looks at me expectantly.

My heart does a flip-flip-flip thing. In my pocket, I grip my pen harder. In front of us, an upturned wheelie bin has spilled its contents, and I walk around it. Rob just walks through the garbage.

People who should stay locked up. Rob's words fly back at me, twist around my heart, only they're now in Chaos's voice. She has also said them—she must have—and I don't like the way it makes me feel.

BAD. It's like the word lights up on my back. The smear that's left of it. I'm good at writing on my back—in any place, really—so the letters can be read. I only started writing the words to cope. And then writing became the best way to communicate. Words are better, written down. People can't pretend you don't have a voice if your voice has physicality.

"People can never change what they are," Rob says, and his voice gets darker. "What they *intrinsically* are. No amount of therapy can really heal them."

I gulp. He can't know. Can't know what I am.

But immediately, all sorts of scenarios unfold in my head. People out here—the Pures—don't like Healed Offenders. Some believe they can never be healed, and all the time, there are stories of both Healed Offenders and Untrustworthies being murdered. I don't know why Untrustworthies, whether they're Offenders or not, Healed or not, are murdered more than Manipulators or Conceiteds or Egocentrics. Or maybe the Manipulators just know how to get away with being bad, and the Conceiteds and Egocentrics know how to… I don't know, use their money to protect themselves from death at the hand of another. Because they have to be rich. Money can buy everything.

But what if Rob is one of those people who murders Untrustworthies because we are poor and looked down upon and marked as different and bad even when we've done nothing wrong? Because we're not also Offenders, usually. I go cold as I think of the way he questioned me earlier, asking me my name and age…like he didn't believe me? Does he suspect I'm a Healed Offender?

And I'm walking alone with him.

I look around.

There's no one else here…just me and Rob. And he's talking about murder. The gruesome murder of a girl. His sister.

Is it a trick? A warning?

He said we're going to the university campus, but I've never been there before. How do I know he's not leading me to some dark alleyway?

But if he kills me, would I just wake up again? A new life in this video game? Or does this one not have the ability to start over? And it is a game, isn't it?

"You probably heard of the case," Rob says. "That man who was in prison for stealing. When he was released, he killed a girl, wanted to be in prison again. That girl was my Steph."

I haven't heard of the case. But he's not expecting me to say anything.

"Murderers are murderers, no matter what treatment they have. One taste of prison, and it's all they're good for."

I speed up. Ahead, a couple walks together. Need to catch them up. Just seeing them there makes me feel safer.

And then there are more people about.

Rob tells me about how he's going to find the man who killed Steph, and he tells me in gruesome detail exactly what he's going to do. I try not to listen.

———

AT THE CAMPUS, I FEEL SAFER. THERE ARE EVEN more people here, and I notice a few girls giving Rob a wide berth. Then I catch a glimpse of us in the window of one of the buildings, a glimpse of myself and Rob. Both with our *Death Becomes* apparel on, and it's the first time I've noted what I'm wearing today. Really noted how awful it looks.

We look like a couple.

And then Rob puts his arm around me.

I stiffen, but don't stop walking.

We enter a building called the Forum, climb some stairs, take a left turn, and another left—and another, so that we're in a room for the seminar. Several people look up. I try to keep breathing, but it's difficult because my chest feels like it's getting smaller, and my lungs are straining, and my ribs are a cage that just wants to hurt me.

"This is my sister," Rob says to everyone in there. "Not the one who died."

What the hell? I freeze and look at him.

Everyone inhales sharply and looks at me. I look at Rob, and I know he has to be an Untrustworthy, to lie like that. I peer at his forehead. I try to see something there, a blemish that would give it all away. But his is as clear as mine.

But he lied. Is our house a house for Lowers? Are Beth and Cassie and Rob… like us? Is the whole of Pennsylvania Road just for Lowers?

After a while, the seminar leader comes in. I feel better with an adult here, but then I realize that all the people here are adults. I wonder if I can really pull off being one.

Rob smiles at me. Then he tells the seminar leader that I'm unable to speak—*what?*—because I was also there when Steph was attacked and that I tried to stop the man who killed Steph, and I was stabbed in the voice box.

Several people gasp.

I feel sick.

I want to disappear.

Be Brave

KIRA, CALM DOWN. YOU'RE WEAVING YOUR
fears and imagination into your interpretation of reality.

Focus on what's really happening.

Come on, I know you can do this.

We can do this.

Be brave.

Help Me

I ESCAPE FROM ROB'S HEAVY ARM TWO HOURS later. He has a lecture. I decide that I don't, somehow persuade him he read my timetable wrong. He tells me to wait for him.

I don't.

I run to the women's toilets on the first floor of the Forum. Inside a cubicle, I whisper frantically for Chaos, but she's silent now.

"Please!" I whimper.

Nothing.

I take out my phone and scroll through the contacts. There's got to be someone I can call. Has to be.

I find a contact for a Glenn on the phone, and there's something about his name that rings a bell. Somewhere. I text Glenn: **HELP**.

I think he's my handler. Not Chaos.

No…no, that's not right, is it? Where did that come from?

But I have got to have a *physical person* who is a handler, haven't I? My task is to reintegrate with society—to blend in—so that no one knows my real identity because that would be too dangerous. People want to hurt me. Of course, it makes sense that I'd have a handler. Someone to contact if things are going wrong.

And they are going wrong. So terribly badly awfully wrong.

And now I'm not thinking of this as a video game. I'm thinking of it as real life.

Real life.

REAL LIFE.

I write the words down hurriedly on the back of my right hand.

And that's right, isn't it?

I groan, yank at my hair until I feel the sweet, hot tips of pain at my roots.

I wait for a reply.

But it doesn't come.

I swallow hard. Blend in. Got to blend in.

I leave the toilets and buy a ham sandwich and a Coke, not because I'm hungry, but because that seems to be what everyone else is doing. I put the sandwich into my bag, and I take a swig of the Coke.

There's a lake on the campus, and I wander toward it, even though rain is now pounding down. My hoodie isn't enough to protect me, and even my back is getting soaked despite wearing Emilia's backpack, but I like lakes because I can get lost in them.

I stare at my reflection in it, how the pounding rain makes it angry.

Then my phone buzzes. I pull it out of my pocket. My sleeves are pushed up now and LONER winks at me as the water makes it run down my arm.

I stare at the phone's screen. My mouth dries.

Not my handler, Glenn. Not anyone in Emilia's contacts. An unknown number.

I open the text.

My heart pounds.

I KNOW WHO YOU ARE, TAYLOR.

Report

WELL, THAT WAS A SHORT REST FOR ME, WASN'T it? Surely you could've just let me sleep?!

Anyway, you've run away. You're shaken up and you've retreated into yourself. You need me more and more now, and I like being needed. Yes, it's very nice.

Right now, we're walking swiftly along Exeter's High Street, past Starbucks and Build-A-Bear Workshop, dodging around people on the flooding pavements. There are people everywhere, and it's still raining heavily. Windy, too. Three umbrellas have turned inside out in the last two minutes. Some of the people under more fortunate umbrellas are looking at their phones: scrolling social media, messaging friends, checking mobile banking as they walk. A few are looking at the news too— although my perception might be a little off, my timings, because maybe they'll actually be doing this later, this evening or even tomorrow, reading articles of how a bomb has gone off in Baghdad, of how Shaun White has withdrawn from the Winter Olympics, and how the South Devon Railway sea wall has collapsed—the storm last night washed it away—just like that! Proper bad storm that was. See, I can tell you more than you even know, could ever know, because I'm you and I'm me and I'm something more.

But Rob knows who you are, Kira. We both know that. And I guess we should concentrate on that.

Rob knows. Rob knows. Rob knows. These words go round and round your head, clouding my head. And he knows what you are, who you are.

He doesn't like murderers.

We can't go back to Pennsylvania Road. But was that house really our home? We never really settled in. What do you think?

Anyway, you won't miss it. Neither will I.

But then you think of the rat, and you think that you will miss that piece of vermin.

But you're wrong. You're always wrong. See? You're Untrustworthy, Kira. You can't trust anything you think. But you can trust me. I'm not just here to make you feel better—to allow you to escape to an alternate reality where you've just had Raven's baby—no, I'm here to help you. To guide you. because I can see clearly and you can't.

Now you start crying. You're homeless. But don't worry. I'll look after you. And I've always looked after you, haven't I?

There's a good spot not far from here, just outside Tesco, down on the corner, good because it's sheltered and it holds some of the day's warmth in it until late into the night—though maybe not in this weather. Two Homeless Men are already there and we watch them carefully. They watch us too, but I tell you that you're safe and so you believe me. Good, isn't it?

We don't have a sleeping bag or a blanket, so we take your sodden hoodie off, squeeze water out of it, then drape it over us. We'll have to use Emilia's backpack—as drenched as it is—as a pillow.

"That ain't going to help, girl," one of the Homeless Men calls out. "You're soaked through."

I wonder why you—and me, by extension—think of them as Homeless Men, as if Homeless is part of their name. Then we realize that if it's their name it's also yours. You're the Homeless Girl. I'm just your help.

I give you a little more activeness now, dialing back my control, and watch as you reach into your bag, retrieve your pen, and try to write HOMELESS on your arm. The pen takes a few seconds to work, bleeds a little, but then you write it in block capitals and underline it because that's the kind of typography the word deserves. All words have their own typography that they prefer to be dressed in, and you're really in tune with their minds—just as I'm in tune with your mind.

And your mind is strange, girl!

Woah, now you're thinking of Rob and that text, and well, so am I. We're back to being we. I like when we're one.

We think of how Rob knows who we are. We picture the house, and it's swarming with police as they look for you: the Untrustworthy who thought she'd live in a Pure area, because even though Rob lied, he can't be a Lower. We wonder what Cassie and Beth think of us now. And Bradley.

Then our phone is in our hand, and we're staring at the text.

"It doesn't mean it's from Rob," I tell you, and in case you don't hear my words, I also try to interject the sentence into your thought stream. But you try and push me out. Girl, you're so weird, sometimes welcoming me, sometimes challenging, fighting. No wonder you've got no friends.

Maybe I shouldn't try too hard to think of us as one and the same.

So, you *settle down to your first afternoon of homelessness. The man was right—your hoodie does nothing to warm you. Makes you colder.*

A little while later, more men arrive. One tries to talk to you. Seems friendly, but you pretend you don't speak English. They start talking among themselves, and you imagine they're saying vulgar stuff about you.

The hairs on the back of your neck rise, and your chest feels heavy. You're breathing too fast, and then you can't stand what the men are saying and you get up.

You run to a new street, splashing and slipping and sliding in the rain, but everything looks so much more frightening in the coming dark. The darkness holds secrets. The darkness hides things. The darkness is danger.

Come on, Kira—I want to scream at you. You finished playing now?

Let's just go back to the house.

We both know who that text was really from.

Bleeding

MY HANDS ARE BRUISED AND BLEEDING WHEN I get back to the house. I haven't got my keys. I don't know what happened to my hoodie or bag. Or my hands. I stare at my skin, under the weak glowing light of the flickering lamppost that casts long, weak shadows.

Then I ring the bell.

Cassie opens the door. "Emilia?"

After she's insisted that I change clothes—supplying me with some of her own—and has blasted my hair with her hairdryer, she has a lot of questions, and I don't know which answers will score me the highest points. I have to keep winning this game. That stint with the homeless, that has to be signifying my drop in rank. A sign of what's to come if I don't score more points, get more coins, spend them in the shop.

And I can't go back there. Those men.

Oh, you're funny.

Chaos is laughing at me, and it's not a kind laugh. It's a hyena's laugh. It's a cactus being rolled up and down my back. She's changed, now we're in the video game. She's unpredictable, getting meaner. It's no wonder though. Having two people in the same body is exhausting. It's draining. It's frightening. And it's lonely.

You wouldn't think it would be, always having someone to talk to, but it's not like that. Chaos is here all the time—I know that—but she doesn't always speak, isn't always accessible to me. When I need her most, I can't be sure she'll help me.

I know I'm different. Because she's here. And she shouldn't be. Normal people don't have someone else in their body.

Or maybe they do, and they just don't tell anyone. Maybe everyone does. Maybe everyone argues with their inner selves. Maybe other people have multiple inner voices.

Maybe I should be lucky I've just got one.

She's exhausting enough.

My New Mother

THAT EVENING, THERE'S A PRIVATE MESSAGE on my Facebook account from Tina Johnson, and a quick look at her profile tells me that she's playing the role of my new mother. She's even got a full Facebook page set up with hundreds of photos and posts. Talk about authentic. No one would ever suspect she was as fake as 'Emilia Johnson' is.

I feel strangely smug as I click onto her message.

Hi Em,
Are you settling in well now? Give us a call. Bobby wants to talk to you. He's got onto the team, but don't tell him I've already told you. Write back as soon as you get this. Let us know you're okay as you didn't phone last night. We were worried, but we know you'll be wanting to go out with your new Exeter

friends. Be careful with all this bad weather though, won't you? xx

I stare at the message for a few minutes. Concern. There's concern in the message. A mother's concern.

Aw, now isn't that nice? Chaos's voice borders on sarcastic, mean, and suddenly I wonder if it's really *my* mother behind the fake Tina Johnson profile—if this has been arranged as a way for me to keep in contact with her, with my real loved ones. I look back through Tina Johnson's profile again, searching for a clue. Then I find it.

It's cleverly hidden away, but in a photo dated two years ago, 'Tina' has taken a photo of her avocado toast. I can see the tablecloth. It is our tablecloth. Blue and white stripes, with a coffee stain that looks like a curled-up cat, though its tail is sticking out more than I remember.

But this is it: my mother's sign to me that it's her. Really her.

Warmth floods me.

I write back so quickly my fingers buzz.

Hi Mum! How lovely to hear from you. It's nice here. I've got great housemates.

And then I'm telling her all about them, and the seminar I went to. And I try to think of something I can really tell her—something that's *me*—and at last I settle on: **I still need to buy a new dictionary.**

It's our ongoing joke. When I was nine—before we found I was an Untrustworthy—I 'borrowed' Dad's dictionary so I could get a little help in a spelling test, and I made the mistake of asking Mum to hold my bag for a moment at the school gates, and she felt the extra weight of it and demanded to know what it was.

Of course, I owned up. Maybe I was still even partly Pure then—because the Untrustworthy part has to grow and take over gradually, doesn't it?—and Mum pulled the dictionary out of my bag, a look of disapproval on her face. And at that exact moment, a seagull flew over us—even though we were pretty far inland—and a huge dollop of bird mess landed on the dictionary. Dad's pride and joy. Mum was so horrified she chucked it right in the rubbish bin at the school gates and told me I needed to save up for a new dictionary for Dad from my pocket money.

I never did save up enough money, and Mum replaced the book herself that same day. Same edition, even bent back the corner of the cover so it matched the crease Dad once complained about. But it's been our ongoing *thing* between us, me and Mum, as Dad never let on if he knew that the dictionary had been replaced. He'd been out at a golf tournament all that weekend and hadn't been due back until the next day. It was—

"Hey, Em. She looks just like you."

I look up at Beth's words, jolted away from my memories.

And that's when I see the face on the TV. The TV? It takes me a moment to realize I'm in the living room, on the sofa, staring at my face. My face on the TV.

The noodles that I hadn't realized I was eating clump in my mouth, and I forget how to chew.

Oh God. They're looking for me. Because I'm a Lower (once a Lower, always a Lower) and someone knows I'm back out here, not in the Lowers' site, but out here in the real world and—

And there are angry people out there. People who want me dead.

And one of them's onto me. The *You're not alone* message was a warning. From one of them, one of Mr. Norman's fans. And the text was confirmation that they know who I am. Kira Taylor. And where I am.

Oh God.

"Ha, you sure you ain't her?" Bradley laughs, and his figure just suddenly materializes next to me. "You dyed your hair to throw us off the scent?"

"Mate, that girl's *missing*," Cassie says, ballooning up from the blue beanbag. "And Em's right here."

"Well, a secret twin then?"

I force out a laugh.

Glenn. I need to speak to Glenn.

I make my excuses and go up to my room. I search for his phone number on Emilia's phone, then on every scrap of paper. But there's nothing. Did I…misremember?

That's because Glenn's not real. Or well, he isn't who you think he is, Chaos says. *You need to remember, girl.*

"Shut up!" I hiss, spinning around. The rat looks at me.

I take a deep breath. I need to go somewhere safer. Like The Facility. There are guards there.

But Mrs. Norman still got in.

"Oh, God. I can't go there!"

Look, Kira. You're safe here. Stay here. I'm just messing with you.

I frown. "Can I trust you?"

Of course you can trust me. I'm all-knowing. I'm the best person you can trust. Now, let me control you for the next few days. I'm getting stronger. I can do this. I'll keep you safe, I promise.

Danger

I AM A GOOD STUDENT. I WRITE YOUR ESSAYS and I attend all your lectures, even if I do sip cheap beer out of our new coffee flask that I keep in our new rucksack—I shoplifted both for you. But every student does that, right? The beer-in-flask and the shoplifting, yes? And I'm here to have fun now, Kira. I'm free. I'm living as a teenager should, and this is exciting.

I even make friends. And not everyone here thinks I'm a total nutcase. I only have to spend one class once a week with the people who think I'm Rob's mute sister, but it doesn't really bother me.

After the last seminar of the day—and we're a few days later now, because it's Monday, your first Monday here, girl!—I sign up to a few societies. English Soc, of course, and Netball. Life Drawing Soc and Disney Karaoke. I'm trying to be more outgoing (and I guess you are, too, now—you can thank me later).

After I've signed up by writing your name (Emilia Johnson—because you still think you're her and my actions have got to be in keeping with your beliefs, at least somewhat) and email address on the sheet, I head over to the campus shop in the Forum. It's a big shop, and it's crowded now. Six o'clock lectures have just finished, and other students are milling about and buying food.

I head to the care aisle and select a box of blond hair dye. It's the shade Emilia Johnson was wearing in some of her Facebook photos from earlier this year, before she evidently started her Goth phase, and I've always wanted to dye my hair blond. Guess I'll have to settle for yours. Ours.

The guy at the checkout gives me a coy smile. "Going to become a wild blond?" *He winks.*

I feel heat rush to my chest. I lean forward and fold my arms on the counter. I dressed this body this morning and I'm wearing a low-cut top I found in Cassie's wardrobe, so now my breasts spill out. Don't worry. I cleaned all the words off your skin, too. It's mine now.

Checkout Guy tries not to drool. Want to know what he's thinking? Sure: Fine pair of knockers. I'd fuck her.

I'm blushing, and that's not just because I know his thoughts. But you'd be attracted to him too, Kira, because he looks like how Raven does in our stories.

"You should come to our party tomorrow night," Checkout Guy says as he takes my money. "I've always had a thing for blond girls." He winks.

I promise that I'll come.

—

MY NEW STUDENT HOUSE IS BUSY WHEN I GET home. Beth has got friends over. I go straight up to the girls' bathroom and read the instructions on the hair dye.

As I follow the instructions, I think of your next assignment and what I'm going to do it on. I start planning it out (and don't worry, you will remember it all photographically, your essay outline, because you have me helping you and don't worry, it's not cheating—he can't prove you're not me).

It takes an hour for me to dye my hair—your hair—but the dye is cheap and the hair has just turned a mousy brown.

There's an uneasiness within you, no matter how much I squash you down, coiled up like a snake. This uneasiness really annoys me—like you're watching me and don't approve. Ha.

I look around. Cassie's vanity case is in the cupboard, and I take it. Inside are tubes of concealer, razor blades, and a pair of scissors with pink handles.

I pick up the scissors.

A couple days after your seventeenth birthday, at The Facility, you were obsessed with scissors. They wouldn't let you use any there, so you drew them on anything you could find and you made their blades bigger and bigger and sharper and sharper. Then you wrote SCISSORS *on your body because you thought it was the perfect metaphor. Something that snips away at paper, cutting it smaller and smaller, until only fragments remain if you go at it long enough.*

There's a glint in my eye now as I hold up the scissors. The scissors wink back at me. I smile.

I take a lock of our freshly dyed hair in my right hand, and with my left I cut it.

Snip.

Snip.

Snip.

Oh, isn't life a lark?

At some point later, Beth knocks on the door. She wants to pee.

I come out.

"Oh my god! Your hair!" she shrieks, and her eyes widen like saucers. She looks behind me, into the bathroom, and I haven't

tidied up very well (sorry, I'm not like you, not a neat freak).

"You did it yourself, Emilia?"

I smile and fluff up what is left of my hair. "Do you like it?"

Beth looks troubled. "I—yes, it's—it's brilliant."

Brilliant. *Interesting word choice. It will do.*

Freddie the rat thinks it's brilliant too. I can tell by the way he watches me—but if you were in the controller's chair, you'd think he was telling you that in his squeaky voice (now, isn't that a clue, Kira?) and then you'd both discuss some pointless and weird topic. But you're not in control—it's me—and while I may be going to a party tomorrow night, I'm still a good student, and I've got an essay to do now. See, don't make me out to be all-bad, Kira!

AN HOUR LATER, AND I'VE WRITTEN YOUR ESSAY and submitted it via the online portal. Then I log onto Facebook on Emilia's account and I find the profile of Checkout Guy. He's called Josh Chester and I learn he's a third-year biology student.

But you like older guys, don't you?

I add Josh as a friend, and I wait for him to accept.

It takes exactly nine minutes and forty-one seconds for the notification to come through that says we are now friends. Then I click on the chat icon.

I'm now a blond bombshell, *I write.*

He replies: You have me throbbing already. Fancy coming over tonight? Don't think I can wait until tomorrow.

I laugh and I feel great. (See, this is fun, isn't it? Feeling sexy and empowered and confident.)

I write back: No, the party's tomorrow, Josh. Tonight I'm being a good girl.

His reply is here in seconds: So you can be bad tomorrow?

I smile. Then I log off (because, take notice, Kira, you've got to play hard to get and can't give a guy everything he wants) and put the laptop away.

I look at Freddie. "How about some dinner? I'll grab us some pizza."

The Party

"YOU KNOW THAT MEME THAT SAYS 'MY friends think I'm quiet, until they get to know me?'" Bradley points at me. "You're exactly like that, Emilia. Right party animal, aren't you?"

I take another swig from the beer can on the coffee table. I think it's Rob's but he's now in the kitchen mixing vodka and lemonade. Cassie's just arrived back with more six-packs and a bag of wine bottles.

"Pre-drinks!" she yells, and I stand up and start sexy-dancing even though AC/DC is blasting out of the speakers by the microwave. I find I like AC/DC.

As a house, we're getting ready to go to Josh's party. Emilia's housemates aren't technically invited, but don't worry, everyone knows it's fun to have strangers turn up at parties. And Josh won't care so long as I go.

Bradley hones in on me, and then we're dancing together. Beth turns the music up, and then Cassie's yelling at me that I need to do my makeup else I won't have time.

I give my newly opened can of beer to Bradley and then Cassie's steering me away to the kitchen where hundreds of tubes and pots are on the table. Cassie studies drama and she's also on the theatre committee. I know that stage makeup is her thing, so I tell her to go as big and bold as possible on my look.

Her cheeks light up and she beams, and then I'm sitting at the table, and the house is pulsing with more music, and she's layering paste after paste onto my face.

"Shut your eyes, Em."

I shut my eyes as she zooms in on me with a fat charcoal pencil.

When I open my eyes, I see I look great for two seconds before Cassie whisks the mirror away and yells for Beth. My eyes are rimmed in black, and my eyelids are all shimmery. My face has never worn so much bronzer, but it works strangely well with my new hair. My hair, yes! Cassie fixed it last night with a bottle of cheap hair dye. It's now platinum blond and my hair has a natural curl to it, extenuated by the short cut that Cassie also tidied up in the late hours.

"Looking hot, babe!" Bradley yells.

I wonder when I became a 'babe.'

———⌣———

WE'RE WALKING TO THE ADDRESS JOSH SENT me this morning. I'm wearing Cassie's little black dress and a pair of red-hot heels from Beth, and the combination works wonders to show off my legs. Seriously, girl, we shouldn't hide these!

I hear Josh's house before I see it because it's a stereo box and people are pouring out of it.

Now, I'm inside the house and an attractive guy is eyeing me up. I thrust my chest out a little more and stick my hip out in what I know is a provocative stance. A slow smile spreads across the guy's face.

But then Josh is here, and he's grabbing my hand, pulling me away.

He gives me a drink and tells me that I look beautiful.

His hand tugs at one of my curls, and, when his fingers brush against my face, a thousand fireworks go off in my body. I lean in toward him, and I smell his citrus aftershave. His eyes are dark and mesmerizing, and they never once leave me as I stand as close as possible, with the tiniest of spaces between our lips. But our lips don't touch…yet.

Remember, girl, playing hard to get is everything.

It's like the two of us are in our own bubble, each of us frozen as the party whirls on around. We are staring at each other, into each other, devouring each other's souls—or the parts of them we can access.

I feel his heartbeat get faster, and I see his pupils dilate with lust.

A thousand seconds stand still. We, me and Josh, are the only people in the world.

Okay, playing hard to get isn't important now. I can change my mind.

No!

My eyes widen. Kira? What the hell? This is my *turn to be in control. You've had this body for years. Go away! Trust me. I know what's best for you.*

And Josh is best for you, me, us. I love him. He replaces Raven and Jase and all the other people in my life. It's only me and Josh.

I'm going upstairs. I stare at the way his shirt stretches tightly over the muscles in his back as he leads me to his bedroom.

Then me and him, we're both on his bed, on the firm mattress, and our lips still haven't touched. But that doesn't matter because we know each other, me and Josh, we recognize each other. Our souls belong together. And our hands are hungry.

No—stop it. Give me control back!

Just fuck off, Kira!

I stare at his bare chest and stomach. His muscles aren't as defined as I was hoping for, but that doesn't matter because it's him, it's Josh, and he's here with me.

He takes my dress off and the air pulses with life as I stare at him, with only my underwear gracing my body.

Stop it! Get out! Get out! Get out! Get out!

Ha.

My lips meet Josh's, and our bodies meet, and my arms are around him, pulling him closer and closer—as if I can get any closer.

Stop!

I want to let him know me, just like how you promised yourself no one would ever know you.

The Struggle

I STARE AT MYSELF IN THE BATHROOM MIRROR. I'm sweating, there's a strange red glow over my face, and huge bags hang under my eyes. And I'm at a party. A God-damn party. I feel anger boiling up within me. Chaos took over. No choice. Couldn't stop her. And she's the forceful part of me, the part with no self-control.

I swallow hard. It's not been like that before. I *could* stop her before. Push her away, right? If I needed to... But she never took over, not like that. She comforted me, reported back what I'd missed when I was too busy panicking.

She'd never taken over my body so forcefully.

A sinister parasite. Killing its host? I feel sick.

"You can't do that again," I say. And she doesn't answer. Of course she doesn't answer. I'm just drunk and talking to myself in the mirror in some guy's bathroom at a freaking house party.

I need to leave.

I splash cold water on my face quickly and then check my dress. It feels twisted, and it's far too short. I have a vague memory of coming to in a hot, sweaty room, peeling myself away from the guy and grabbing my dress as I ran out, ignoring his angry shouts as I locked myself in here. Now, even with my dress on, I'm showing too much cleavage and too much leg. Clear skin, my words gone.

A jacket, I need a jacket. But I know I didn't bring one. Chaos didn't bring one.

A moment later, I open the bathroom door. A girl rushes in past me, and I hear the sounds of her throwing up. It's dark up here, but there are more bodies moving and couples canoodling. I can hear people having sex.

I try not to think about what my body nearly did when I wasn't in control.

"Emilia?"

It's Beth. Beth looking concerned.

"You all right?" She pulls me to the side. "You don't look so good."

I shake my head. "I'm going home."

She nods. "Give me a sec and I'll grab Cassie and see where the boys are at."

Beth disappears.

People are looking at me strangely.

I see one girl pass a packet of white powder to another.

Someone offers me a small yellow tablet. I shake my head.

"Where the hell did you go?"

I look up, and it's Josh. He's barely wearing anything, and his eyes glint with a ferocity that reminds me of his anger as I ran.

"Come on." He tries to pull me back to his room again, but I shake my head and resist and—

I vomit over him.

He looks at me in disgust.

He backs away.

I feel strange.

I need to look for Beth and Cassie.

I find them downstairs. Cassie is attached to a boy at the mouth, and Beth slowly detaches her from him.

Then we're outside, and I think some time has passed but I'm not sure, because everything's happening in fragments.

We get home. My head hurts.

"Has she taken something?"

I sit down at the kitchen table. Cassie's makeup is still spread out on it, and I find a hand mirror. I pick it up. My eyeliner is in streaks, and I have never seen my eyes so haunted.

I Don't Like This

I SCRUB MY BODY HARD IN THE BATH, FEELING sick. Sicker than I thought was possible. My head pounds.

I don't like this game.

I need to get out.

I turn round and round, trying to see the 'end game' button. On the mirror, the walls, the sink. It's not there, but it's got to be somewhere.

I don't like this game, and I don't want to play it anymore.

I press my fingers into the fat on my left thigh, watch how it wobbles. Pain thrums through me.

"Get out," I mutter. My throat burns with the sound of my own voice, and my stomach churns.

Need to get out. Get out of this world and back to…

Back to my bedroom, in my house with Mum and Dad and Brooke.

Before all this started.

"I don't want to play anymore!" I look up at the light. Are they watching me? The game-makers. They have to be. It wouldn't be ethical, safe, if they weren't. And I need to get out. They need to take me out of the game.

"I resign!" I yell.

"Emilia?" Cassie's voice, outside. "Are you okay?"

My heart speeds up. Another player. Wait—no, I *thought* she was another player, but what if she's just part of the game, another figment of it? Or a part designed to keep me in here? Yes.

"I'm fine!" I shout. "Sorry." Because she can't come in here. She can't see the fear on my face, my desperation to get out.

I look around. A pen. I need a pen. Maybe the game-makers can't hear me. Maybe they need a visual sign. I need to write a note. I stretch my legs out, my canvas. But I haven't got a pen. Need a pen.

I get out of the bath, sloshing soapy water everywhere, and rummage through the cabinets. Lotions and ointments, all of them gloopy and messy, and I can't write a note with them properly. Need something to make clear shapes, clear marks.

My gaze falls on Cassie's disposable razor. The pack of refills next to it.

Yes.

I grab the box, take out a brand-new blade.

I turn it over and over in my hands.

I stare at the fineness of it. The sharpness.

I touch it to the pad of my thumb, slowly.

I press it. The tiniest of pressures.

But a thin red line appears.

No!

Chaos. I jolt.

I'm sorry!

But Chaos isn't sorry. She's never sorry. She took my body. She controlled me, worked against me. She nearly made me do stuff. Stuff that wasn't me, made me nearly break my promise.

I wouldn't have actually done it, I promise! I just wanted to have fun!

It wasn't fun. I don't like this game!

I was helping you! I really thought I was.

But she hasn't helped me. Chaos hasn't helped me. And then I yell at her to shut up, and she does, but Cassie's shouting again, and I can hear other voices too—Rob's and Beth's.

I stare at the blade.

I press it deeper into my thumb, until redness pours out, like a waterfall. But it doesn't hurt.

I don't feel anything.

And that's the most wonderful part of all because it means I'm actually in the game. I can't get hurt, no matter what I think happens here, and soon I'll be out of here. I just have to write the command so the game-makers can see and understand.

My game is over, and I am getting out.

Waiting

THE NEXT MORNING, THERE IS A MAGPIE ON my windowsill, and it pecks at the rotting wood. I watch it, strangely fearful.

I am still trapped in the game.

It didn't work. The game-makers didn't get my message. Or they did, but they ignored it.

"You'll just have to win the game then," Freddie the rat tells me, as he picks seeds out of his food bowl and eats them noisily. I don't remember feeding him.

I don't want to play the game.

But I have no choice. I must have signed up for this...or Chaos did.

So, I have to play. I have to do what they want.

Two People

WE ARGUE A LOT NOW. ME AND CHAOS.

She used to be kind. But she's not now. She's different. She used to help me. She'd tell me stories, whisk me away all those times when Mr. Norman was hurting Brooke so I didn't have to think about it. Chaos was on my side, and she'd tell me stories that I loved. Stories where I was successful. Stories where I wasn't an Untrustworthy.

We were like one person then, even though there were two of us. And Brooke, too. Three girls twisted together. Chaos *saw* Brooke, and Chaos told me. Chaos and I were on the same side.

But it's not like that anymore. And the last few days since she took over my body have been awful. She hasn't taken over again—hasn't made me do stuff—but she's just there. This *thing* inside me who no longer wants to be there. Who fights me. Who wants to have more control, because she liked controlling me before.

Most times, I can still push her voice away. I can shut her up.

But we're in competition with each other now, and if I slip up, then I know she's going to rear up. She'll eagerly take my place, take my body again.

It's Valentine's Day today, too, and I know she wants to go out on the pull. I can feel that in her. She's stronger now—I can feel her like this army inside me. If she takes control, I don't know if I'll get my life back.

And maybe the worst part is that I don't want my life back.

She is an Insect

I KEEP A LOW PROFILE AT THE WEEKEND, THEN head to my lectures on Monday, and I try to concentrate on them. But it's difficult when I'm also trying to concentrate on not letting her in, and not even allowing her to speak. It was easier at the weekend; drinking another bottle of gin I found by Freddie's cage helped, but I can't be drunk at university. And she's fighting me, today. I can feel her, this force, this pressure in my head.

I listen to what Dr. Michaels says about feminism in pop culture, and Chaos is listening too. I've got to listen and concentrate on what Dr. Michaels is saying and also concentrate on the wall. The wall I've built in my head. The wall around Chaos.

But Chaos has got a hammer, and she's trying to knock it down, and each blow of the hammer makes me flinch, makes my head feel looser, like the shell's going to break away into a thousand pieces any moment now and then everything inside me will splatter out. Maybe the other students around me will see Chaos, her physical form.

She'll look like an insect. I suddenly know that with clarity. A huge insect, about a foot long. She'll be made from soft metal with a fudge-like appearance, and her shape will be a black beetle, but with super-long antennae. Her eyes will be metallic and shiny and round, and she'll be one of those beetles that eats everything. Because she wants to consume and consume and consume.

"Hey, Emilia!" A red-haired girl falls in step beside me. The lecture's finished and we're outside. "You want to partner up for that research project?"

"Sure," I say, though I don't know what project she's talking about. I don't remember a research project. But then again, I don't remember the lecture. I curse under my breath; I was concentrating so hard on not letting Chaos speak to me that I didn't really take in Dr Michaels's words.

The red-haired girl—Mandy, I think her name is Mandy—gives me a strange look, and I realize that I must've cursed loudly.

"Don't worry," Mandy says. "It's not due in for another week. We've got plenty of time."

"Yeah. Okay." I nod. The rest of my day is free. "Do you want to start it now?"

She does—she's one of those people who always hands her assignments in as early as possible, I can tell—and we head off to the library.

It turns out Mandy is an excellent partner to have for a research project because she's the kind of person who takes control and delegates tasks, and then watches you intently while you do the task. We sit at a computer—two of us squeezed into one space at the side of the Forum Library—and she leans back and watches as I navigate the search directories.

"No, that journal's no good. I saw something about it that questioned its credibility. And Miss Meyers doesn't like that."

"Miss Meyers?"

She smacks a hand to her chin. "Gill. Gill Meyers. God, I *still* keep forgetting that you can call the lecturers and seminar leaders by their first names. Weird, isn't it? Not like I'm a second-year student or anything!"

Very weird.

Shut up!

I shove Chaos back behind her brick wall, but she's pushing hard. My eyes start to water, and then I can hear cracking, and the bricks, no! Not the bricks. I try to hold them in place, and my vision blurs.

Mandy doesn't even notice the fight going on inside me. All that's important to her is that we get a first on our research paper. If we don't, she won't be working with me again.

But I'll be working with you.

Memories

I WALK QUICKLY HOME. IT'S GETTING DARK, and the dark makes me uncomfortable. I imagine all sorts of bad things that could happen to me, and when a man starts following me, I think it's the end, and my teeth chatter incessantly, and I wonder what I'll do when he grabs me. In my dreams, when this happens, I always freeze. Just freeze. Can't scream. Can't do anything.

When Mr. Norman grabbed Brooke, she didn't scream. And, after a while, when she knew fighting wouldn't get her anywhere, she didn't do anything. She just…let him.

But this man behind me is walking faster and faster and faster, and he's going to kill me. I look around. There's no one else here. No one else at all and—

Let me take over. Let me help you.

I stiffen, speed up. My breath fogs the night air. How did it get dark so quickly? Were Mandy and I really working on that research paper for hours? Did we eat dinner? Did we eat anything? I can't remember. There's a gap. A huge gap.

I can tell you what happened.

I shove Chaos back behind her wall and grab my house keys from my pocket. I clench them in my fist, so a key sticks out between each finger.

The man's steps are heavy, loud.

I glance behind me, my heart pounding.

He's tall. Looks broad-shouldered. Got a hood up. Can't see his face.

He gets closer.

I'm slowing down…no, can't slow down! Mustn't, and—

And he's next to me and—

The man overtakes me.

He doesn't attack me.

I run to the house and only stop panting when I'm safely up in my room and Freddie's telling me he'll protect me.

The Man

THE NEXT AFTERNOON, A MAN FOLLOWS ME again. The same man? I don't know.

I've just stepped out of a lecture on Elizabeth Barrett Browning, and already there's a man following me, literally on campus. I noticed him as soon as I left the auditorium, because he was standing opposite the door and his hood was up. He was dressed all in black, but as soon as I looked at him—directly at him—he seemed to disappear. Just vanished into the sudden crowd of students who were waiting for the lecture changeover.

I didn't think of anything more of it, of that man—until now. I'm walking toward Pennsylvania Road, and he's behind me. About twenty yards. But he's definitely following me.

I've taken two roundabout routes already, going round in circles, and he's still onto me.

But I feel strangely calm. It's the gin I was sipping all through that lecture. I'm sure. It's making me too calm.

Oh, you silly girl.

I walk a little faster, and then my house is on the right—for the third time. Yes. I've been walking round and round.

I look toward the windows, but I know that I can't go in because the man following me can't know where I live. What I need is for Cassie or Beth or Bradley or even Rob to look out of the window, to see me being followed and to come and help me.

And I know I shouldn't rely on others to help, not when I'm in danger, but I can't think of what else to do. Even if this man doesn't appear to want to hurt me—he just follows me and nothing else—because I was stupid earlier and led him through a dark alleyway where it was just us two, alone.

But he didn't hurt me.

But he's following you.

Help. Help. Help.

I WALK FOR TWO HOURS BEFORE BRADLEY twigs what's going on. I've walked past our house eight more times and five of those times Bradley was at his window. His desk is at his window, and I know he sketches the people who walk past. I worried that it was too dark though, now, for him to notice me. To notice the man.

HELP. HELP. HELP.

Woah, where did that come from?

But I don't answer Chaos, just watch those words—my words—float away on the breeze. And then I'm two streets away and then Bradley's here in his car—a car I think I vaguely knew he had—throwing the door open, and I climb in. I feel victorious, like I've escaped the stalker—and I'm happy. And I did it all on my own. I faced reality, I didn't hide.

I didn't need Chaos inside me. I can figure out how to get out of this game by myself.

The Police

"I THINK WE SHOULD GO TO THE POLICE,"
Cassie says, when Bradley and I arrive back.

I feel scared now. The strange haziness I was in has worn
off.

"Yeah," Beth says. "There's that nutter wandering around.
What's his name? Barry Norman?"

My mouth dries.

………………… isn't he….

The world stops.

……………………………dead?

I stare at them.

I wait for Chaos to chime in, to say that she changed what
I heard Beth say to scare me, made me hear something else.
Or that I heard it wrong.

Only Chaos doesn't say anything.

Chaos is quiet.

She's listening, and she's as scared as I am—I feel her fear, so sudden.

"Wh—what did you say?" I can hardly breathe. "Barry Norman?"

Cassie's face starts to wobble and blur, and then it's the whole kitchen blurring, and Beth's face is twisting up.

"Yes."

I hear her voice, but it echoes. She's far away.

"Haven't you seen the police reports? That murderer escaped from prison and they're worried because one of those poor girls he was abusing went missing at the same time. That girl, Brooke Taylor, I think her name is? Her uncle's desperate to find her."

I feel sick. Their faces are still swimming and changing. And then Beth's hair is getting shorter and her face rounder and her eyes smaller and then Barry Norman is in the kitchen and he's laughing because I killed him yet he's somehow alive.

You're not alone.

The Promise

I MAKE IT TO MY ROOM AND LIE DOWN ON THE floor. My heart pounds. Barry Norman. Out there. Alive.

Not dead.

"Help me!" I shout at Chaos, but she's not answering. Not there?

You're alone.

I'm alone. Why am I saying 'you're'? It's just me. Not Chaos this time. Oh, God.

And Barry Norman is out there.

I need Chaos to take over to control me—and I don't care whether we go to more parties or whether I have sex with men like Josh. I don't care. Because men like Josh aren't men like Barry Norman. And Chaos will keep me safe.

But Chaos doesn't come.

It's just me. Alone.

He promised I never would be. And I am.

And I hate it.

I pick up a pen.

HELP ME.

Therapy

TRY HARDER. THAT'S WHAT MY SEMINAR leader is telling me. Jack Bates. I'm in his office now—I signed up yesterday for a slot of his office hours, right before the Elizabeth Barrett Browning lecture—and we're both looking at my first assignment feedback. It's for an essay I do not remember writing.

"I understand that changing university mid-degree can be quite a change. Quite disruptive. But if you could just engage a little more in seminar debates, it would really help. Remember 15 percent of this credit is based on your seminar interaction."

But it's hard to interact when I can't speak. Can't bring myself to, anymore. Not in front of all those people. I'm doing better at home, with Beth and Cassie and Bradley— and sometimes I even manage to verbally ask Rob to pass the saltshaker or inquire as to whether there are any letters for me. But I can't speak anymore in front of fifteen students whom I don't know. And none of them expect me to. They ignore me, for the most part. And there's a group project coming up, and I know that every single one of them is praying they don't get landed with me. Maybe even Mandy. We didn't get a first on our project.

"Are you still having therapy, if you don't mind me asking?" Jack asks.

Therapy? No.

No therapy.

Never had therapy.

Yes. You have.

I frown.

"Emilia?" Jack prompts.

And then I realize he's talking about Emilia, not me, and there must be some record of therapy or something in Emilia's file. But why would they make my new persona have something…wrong with her?

My eyes travel to the bookcase behind him. Lots of theory and criticism books, and some graphic novels. And a box. A box for a board game. Snakes and Ladders.

I stare at it for the rest of the appointment, trying to make sense of this all—and, most of all, how can the man I killed be alive?

No Sign

"THAT MAN'S STOPPED FOLLOWING YOU?" Cassie asks.

I nod. I think so. I can't think. "There's been no sign of him."

But I'm sure what I say is true, because the words just sort of stagger out of my mouth.

We're in the living room. I'm sprawled on the sofa, sort of reading—at least, there's a book in my lap—but my main focus is on the pen in my hand and the words I'm inking on my skin. I don't even try and hide it now. Cassie's leaning against the doorway that leads to the kitchen. Upstairs, Rob's got a girl in his room.

They're not quiet.

"You sure?" Cassie asks. "I mean, if that guy is still following you, you need to be careful." She pushes her hair over her shoulder. "We all do."

"It's fine."

Cassie moves closer, then pulls a face. "You stink of booze."

"Do I?" I shrug. There's a warm feeling in me, but I can't really remember drinking anything. Not recently. Not in the last day or so. But time keeps doing that weird, blurry thing now.

"Just be careful, Em," Cassie says. "I've got to get to lacrosse practice now. But be careful."

Haughty

THE RAT IS TALKING TO ME AGAIN. HE'S MORE talkative now though, than he ever has been, telling me about his wife and children. How he's the breadwinner of the family. I don't know what the heck he's going on about though because there's only him in the cage. Him, with his beady eyes and haughty face.

Haughty face…

I frown. Something was haughty.

Something to do with…

Pain flashes through me, like it's dissecting my eyeballs and then carving into the soft crevices of my brain. I wince. Clear head. Need a clear head.

"Get some fresh air," the rat tells me. "You're not listening to a word I'm saying."

Fresh air. Yes. Good idea, Freddie.

I head downstairs. Grab a coat. Think it's Beth's. She won't mind. She's nice, like that.

The sun is out for once, and the rain's finally stopped, but it is cold. I don't like the cold sun. Don't like much weather though, not when I think about it, not when—

"Cool tattoos," a deep voice says.

I look up, find I'm about to crash right into a man and—

"It's you."

I freeze, and his hand shoots out, grabs my arm, as if to stop me from falling over. And it's him. All this time, it's been *him*.

It wasn't Barry Norman following me. It was Raven.

They're a Bit Soft Now

RAVEN LAUGHS, AND THEN WE'RE TALKING.

Talking and talking and time blurs, and he takes me to his house. Well, he calls it a house, but it's not really. It's just a garden, an abandoned garden with a summerhouse in. The door's open already, and we step in. Something shifts about on the floor, and I jump back.

Raven laughs. "That's just Dilly."

I stare at the girl on the floor, at her big wide eyes as she stares up at me.

"We need privacy, Dilly," Raven says, then jerks his head toward the rest of the garden.

The girl unwinds herself, and it fascinates me watching her, seeing her unravel her arms and legs—and she seems to get taller and taller, until she's towering above me. Yet she seemed so little on the floor.

Raven clears his throat as she leaves, then he shuts the doors, enclosing us in the stale smell of sweat and alcohol.

"You live here?" I ask, feeling heat rushing to my face.

"Nice spot, innit?" He grins, then readjusts the woolly hat—not so that it reveals his branding though, of course. "Never thought I'd be inviting you here. You were that goody-two-shoes at school. And what are the chances of you turning up here? Come on, Brooke, take a seat."

"It's *Emilia* now," I hiss at him. And why the hell would he purposefully use my sister's name? Unless he never bothered to learn which of us was which. Just saw us as the twins even though we weren't even identical?

He looks vaguely amused as he sprawls out on the leaking pouffe. "So, you're serious about that name then?"

"Of course." Are you mad? But I don't say that last bit aloud. Something stops me.

Because you know?

Know what?

"Sit down, *Emilia*." He smirks.

I sit on the fold-up chair. It creaks, and I'm significantly higher up than Raven is, and I'm very aware of it.

"Biscuit?" He reaches around behind him and produces a half-empty pack of gingernuts. "They're a bit soft now, but still edible."

I decline and pat my pockets, search for a pen that isn't here. HUNGER tries to write itself on my arm in ink only visible to me.

I look around, mainly at the rubbish in here. The empty crisp packets. Flattened beer cans. Two seemingly empty plastic carrier bags hung up on the wall.

"You live here?"

Raven makes an uh-huh noise and smiles to himself.

A tingly feeling works itself up my nose, and I want to bring Raven back to the house. And that girl, too—Dilly. Because she must be one as well. And this is what happens if you're Untrustworthy and don't go to the Lowers' area. Oh, God. And Raven and Dilly aren't even Offenders and they're still treated like this, ousted by society, because of The Detector Room. It's disgusting. My stomach coils, and the stench of stale sweat does nothing to help it.

I try to look around for something nice to comment on. But everything's broken or old and covered in rubbish. I spot a condom wrapper on the floor and hurriedly look away.

"So, what's been happening with you?" Raven asks. "I mean you're obviously doing well. You're at uni. Even considering everything."

Like my Offender status—even though they say it's gone, I can still feel it. My shoulders tighten.

He's going to ask about the Bad Stuff. He's going to ask about the Bad Stuff. He's going to ask about the Bad Stuff.

Want me to take over?

No.

Oh, come on, there's no need to be like that. I was just having fun before, making your new friends like you more. If it wasn't for me, they'd all think you are a right loser.

I take a deep breath and look at Raven. "I'm studying English."

Let me have some fun again! Let me out! Have you any idea how boring it's been for me these last years? Just doing narration and being good. That's so bloody boring! Let me have some fun. We're both in the same body, so why do you get to be the one in charge all the time?

Raven grunts. "Books and books and more books. Such a swot, weren't you." But he's smiling so I don't think he means it in a bad way. Then he leans forward. "I heard you were at that secure unit for—"

I cut him off quickly. "Yes, but I can't talk about it. I'm not her anymore. We can't talk about that."

"Okay." He draws the word out. "So, why'd you call yourself Emilia now?" he asks. "Is that some kind of…safety thing for you? To be someone else?"

"Yes."

"You get a fresh start? Because everyone knows your old name?"

I nod. It's hot in here with the doors shut, and I'm starting to sweat. I look out the glass pane. It's cracked, and it divides the overgrown garden into two. Just like how everything in this world is divided into two. Them and Us. The Pures and the Bad Ones. Cities for us, and cities for them. Raven and Dilly haven't been given new identities, permission to live in Exeter though—they can't have been. They're brave, trying to live undetected in a Pure city.

"That why you dyed your hair, too? Hmm. It does make you look different."

I nod.

"You don't look like an *Emilia*."

"Well, you'll have to get used to it."

"Will I?" There's a challenge in his eyes. "Going to be seeing a lot of you, am I?"

I stare at him. He just laughs softly. I think of Raven and Dilly. I imagine them together in here. I start to feel sick.

"I have to go." I stand up quickly.

"Br—Emilia? You've only just got here."

"I've got stuff to do."

And what am I thinking, hanging out in here with Raven—with an Untrustworthy? You hear about police evicting them all the time, escorting them to the Lower sites. If I'm caught here, trespassing on whoever's garden this is and they realize who I am, that I was previously an Offender, they're going to send me back. And I can't go back to The Facility. I can't be locked in there. Not when Mrs. Norman knows where it is.

Out here, I'm free. I'm hidden.

I have to make sure it stays that way.

I rattle the door handle, try to push the door open, but it won't budge.

Raven stands up next to me, and I'm very aware of his body next to mine and being in here alone with him, and on view, too, through this cracked window, for all the world to see. He grabs the door handle, turning it and giving the bottom of the frame a kick at the same time. The door opens, and fresh air buffets me.

Run!

I run.

Why?

IN THE SAFETY OF MY ROOM, I WRITE A university assignment and try to make it take my mind off Raven and how stupid I was. But at some point, I stop typing on my laptop about Freud and how his theories can be applied to modern literature, and I start writing on my arms.

STUPID. RECKLESS. CARELESS. OFFENDER. WHY.

And then the words take over, writing themselves on me, over and over again, without me even holding the pen. They're just appearing, like someone keeps pressing 'paste' on a once-empty Word document, and they're overlapping, making ugly scribbled areas on my arms that I can't read. But they keep appearing until my heart rate's lowered significantly.

And then the pen falls onto my desk, and I stare at the mangled mesh of words on me, and there's a word underneath it all that's trapped, and that word is *me* and I'm held in place by STUPID and RECKLESS and CARELESS and OFFENDER and WHY, just like that poor word is, and I don't even know what the word really says—who it is, underneath all the ink—because everything gets lost and replaced by labels, until everything becomes the thing that others see it is; and there's never any escape from that. Even when I'm Emilia, I still feel like me. An Untrustworthy. And I still act like one. Emilia wouldn't have gone off with Raven. Emilia would've been careful.

But I'm not.

I'm STUPID and RECKLESS and CARELESS and OFFENDER and WHY, whoever I am.

I curse Raven. It's his fault. His fault for following me.

His fault for reminding me of who I am, what I am.

Angry tears force their way into my eyes.

His fault.

Nightmares

I WISH IT WASN'T RAVEN IN THE STORIES Chaos and I wrote. Because now he's here. And now every time I think of him, it's Story Raven I think of. Not the real him.

The real Raven lives in the summerhouse in the abandoned garden and isn't in love with me.

He's a different person. I have to remember that.

Pretense

I DREAM OF THE DETECTOR ROOM.

You know, I'm just wondering when you're going to stop this pretense. You know The Detector Room isn't real, right? We're not living in some dystopian society and you're not in a video game. No. You've seen too much of The Hunger Games *and* Divergent.

No, I *read* them. They're books. I haven't seen the films.

Whatever. You're still lying to yourself.

No—I'm not. The Detector Room is real. It chewed me up and spat me out into the life of an Untrustworthy the first time, then it chewed me up and spat me out here.

But it's not real. It's all in your head. You've got a strange way of looking at things. I didn't realize the extent that this was affecting you before—and neither did the rehabilitation center. Monika suspected—

Shut up, Mallory.

Mallory? I'm not Mallory. You're getting confused again. Mallory was your friend at school. The one who turned against you. Remember, Kira?

I'm not Kira.

Kira. Brooke. Emilia. Alana. Jane. Who cares what your name is? I certainly don't. And I really wish you'd at least try— because filling your head with all this nonsense about the Detector Room and the branding and the Offenders at De Hewitt—you're just feeding your condition. None of that was real and you have to accept it.

But it was real. I know it was. I don't know why Chaos is lying to me.

I'm the Parasite

SOMEWHERE IN THE FUTURE, YOU'RE CRYING IN your cell because you know then that none of this was real. That it was all me. That I'm the parasite pretending to keep you safe.

They're Real, Aren't They?

"BRADLEY, THE DETECTOR TESTS ARE REAL, aren't they?"

He gives me a strange look. From the bags under his eyes and the mountain of research papers on the kitchen table, I'd guess he's been up all night working on some assignment. "Of course. You're here, aren't you? Why?"

"Nothing." I shrug. "I just had a strange dream last night, and it made me confused."

I smile and go back to my room.

See? I say the word silently, triumphantly to Chaos.

Oh my God, Kira!

BUT YOU HAVEN'T PROVEN ANYTHING. YOU'RE doing it again. Imagining what you want to hear and see and learn. And more and more now you need me to tell you what's going on. What's really going on. So, here's what happened in in the kitchen with Bradley:

You sauntered in, looking the worse for wear. There were big dark circles under your eyes, and you didn't smell great. There was also the world REBEL peeking out from under your left sleeve as you'd pushed it up slightly. Bradley noticed the EL and it confused him. He thought it was a tattoo. A girl's name. Annabel.

"You all right?" He glanced at you and nearly poured too much milk into his bowl. He doesn't like his cereal swimming, just slightly moist is best.

"Bradley," you said, "the exam results are real, aren't they?"

See? Exam results. *Not The Detector Room testing and all that shit.*

"The exam results?" he said.

"The ones that get us into university."

"Of course. You're here, aren't you? Why?"

"Nothing." You shrugged. "I just had a strange dream last night."

So, Kira or Brooke or whatever your name is, that *was what happened. Don't you see how concerning it is when you interpret things differently—when, in your head, completely different conversations have taken place? Don't you see? You're lying to yourself without even knowing, constructing this whole dystopian world and video game shit to justify the suffering you went through, the abuse that happened. I thought the construction was kind of cute at first. Thought you were just putting it on, and that's why I got you out of De Hewitt.*

But it's concerning now. I shouldn't have got you out.

But I got out because I passed The Detector Room.

No, you got out because I took over for you and you were deemed of sound mind and had shown significant progress.

But you're not better. You're getting worse. And I think you need to go back there and—

Vulnerable and Alone

NO! I'M NOT GOING BACK!

And then—then she's silent and I know. I know she's turned against me. She—because she's not part of me. She can't be. Not when she's turned against me. Chaos—Mallory, whatever her real name is. She's probably been Mallory all along. Wanting revenge for my sister supposedly copying her work. Chaos/Mallory has been lying to me. And now she's turned against me—although I shouldn't be surprised. If she's lied to me about her name all this time, then what else is she lying about? Why should I trust her? She just wants me to be vulnerable and alone.

VULNERABLE and ALONE appear on my arm.

Why? Why does she want me vulnerable and alone?

Because I am bad, and she doesn't want to help me. She knows what I am. What I was. She's even been calling me Kira—*and* Brooke, to mess with me, make me more vulnerable. It's not right.

She's against me. She's going to make me go back.

I have to get her out of my head. Get rid of her.

Kill her.

Ridiculous

YOU CAN'T KILL ME.

> *I'm the rational part of you.*
>
> *I'm the part of you that keeps you safe.*
>
> *Don't be ridiculous.*
>
> *I'm you now.*

You're Wrong

"YOU'RE WRONG," I SCREAM, AND I CAN'T STOP the words bursting from me with all this force. "You're not part of *me*. You never were. You just were there, another person trapped in my body suddenly."

I was there for you when you needed me most!

"Maybe you should've been there more for Brooke—when she needed you. Maybe she wouldn't be dead, right now, if you'd looked after her."

Oh, dear. You really aren't well, are you? Look, you're getting so confused. You need me—and it's classic denial to pretend that you don't.

Pain breaks out behind my eyes, and I feel sick.

Chaos is messing with me. She's trying to make me think I'm insane. Chaos is dangerous. No, more than that—she's been lying to me. She made me think *I* had killed Mr. Norman. She narrated a funeral to me, made it all up and made me think it was real—but she made a mistake. My parents wouldn't have gone to that man's funeral. She told me what they wore—but it can't have been.

Unless that was Brooke's funeral?

My head pounds. Am I mixing them up? This is all just too much.

But there is one thing I do know: if Chaos is me and I'm Untrustworthy, then she is too. She's lying. She's making me scared.

I don't know what's real and what's not.

No. *I'm* the one who sees the truth. I am.

You're Funny, Kira

ARE YOU SURE? BECAUSE YOU'RE NOT, ARE YOU? And you'll never really know. Always second-guessing yourself, doubting yourself. Are you having fun? It's fun, isn't it?

The Letter

TIME HAS PASSED—I KNOW THAT, BUT I don't know what happened in it or exactly how much time has passed since we argued, me and Chaos.

It's dark now, though, out the window—but it might be a different day. I can see my reflection in the glass over the inkiness. I'm on my bed, sitting, holding a letter. My hair is a mess. All blond spikes at angles. My chest aches, and I look down at my hands, but my vision blurs. I see words on my skin and the letter, but I can't read them.

"What have you done?" I hiss at Chaos, but she's silent. I can't feel her. What has she made me do since we argued? I shake my head. I don't know. I don't know anything.

I shake my head and I want to scream. My breaths come in short, sharp bursts, and I stare at the letter as it slowly comes back into focus. The pristine paper, the careful penmanship.

My dearest darling Brooke.
I know where you are, and I know what you did.
I'm watching you.
The dark, dark woods are bad.
I think you should start running. Don't you?
I'd sign my name, but you know who I am.

The words blur. My heart pounds. My throat closes up. This—no! I drop the letter, but it just falls into my lap, still touching me.

I'm watching you.

My fingers are shards of ice, yet I'm sweating, and the room is so hot.

I'm watching you.

I turn slowly and the chair creaks—what? I'm sitting on the chair by the desk now? I jump. I look around my room quickly, looking for him because he...

But the only thing that watches me is the rat.

The rat. With its beady little eyes.

The rat has to go. It's him. He's the spy. The rat. It's not real. Not a real animal. It's a robot. And it's been watching me.

Revulsion fills me at the sight of what it's seen. Me. Naked. Me. Screaming. Me. Cr—

There's a knock at my door.

I whimper, but then Bradley's voice comes through it.

"Em? We're going to that party now. Sure you don't wanna come?"

"Sure." My voice shakes. What party? What conversations have I missed? How much life has happened without me?

There's a pause, and I wait for him to leave, wait for the sounds of his footsteps. Wait and—

"Are you okay, Em?"

I stare at the letter. *I'm watching you.*

"Yes," I say, my voice shrill. It doesn't sound like me.

"Okay. See you later then." His footsteps disappear.

I'm Watching You

I FISH OUT ONE OF ROB'S MASSIVE T-SHIRTS from the laundry basket and then wrap it around the rat's cage, so the spy can't see out, and then I leave the house. The letter is folded into my back pocket and after a moment of walking with the cage, I wish I hadn't put it there. Because now the hand that wrote the letter is on my backside. *His* hand.

The hand I vowed would never touch me again.

Me. He touched *me*.

No…he…it was Brooke.

Nausea rips through me, but I try to remain calm, try to keep breathing. But everywhere I look, I see him. The old man walking the dog is Mr. Norman. The woman pushing the pram is Mr. Norman. The boy at the desk of the newsagents is Mr. Norman.

I walk faster, faster, faster. My arms burn under the weight of the cage and the rat's moving about in it, constantly changing the center of gravity because he knows what I'm doing and he needs to make it hard for me.

I curse loudly.

"Brooke?"

I whirl around, breathing hard, ready to throw the cage at the person and—

It's Raven.

"What?" My eyes narrow. My breath comes out in sharp bursts.

"What are you doing?" His dark hair falls into his eyes as he looks down at the cage. "Hey, that's not—" He lifts up the corner of Rob's shirt, revealing the spy. "Is he ill?"

I stare at Raven. My legs feel wobbly.

"Brooke? Is he ill—you taking him to a vet?"

"Don't call me that!" I hiss. "Why would you call me that?"

Raven frowns. "Sorry, I forgot." He looks at me for a long moment, his eyes narrowing.

I'm watching you.

I turn my head instinctively, look around. Look at the people about us, and there are more. There are suddenly so many potential Mr. Normans everywhere.

"Are you okay? What are you doing with Freddie out here?"

"How do you know his name?"

"You told me," he says.

"I didn't." I'm breathing hard. "He has to go."

"Go?"

He's a spy. A spy. A spy. But I can't say the words because I don't think I can trust Raven now, and my hand itches to write that word on me—SPY—to make it real.

"I've got to go," I say, and I hurry off.

Raven doesn't follow.

I walk to the canal. To the lonely part where no one is.

You get ready to throw the rat's cage into the water.

"No—no I don't," I whisper angrily, and I don't know why I say that, when I want to scream at her. But Chaos is back. She's got explaining to do, questions to answer, yet, I can't even speak them now.

My lips aren't mind.

Oh, come on! Yes, you do throw the rat's cage into the water. This was your idea. Now hurry up and do it. It's cold out here.

Murderer

I FEEL AWFUL. BUT I WALK HOME. WITHOUT the cage. Without Freddie.

MURDERER, MURDERER, MURDERER,

I need to write the word, but I can't.

Uncle Glenn

YOU WERE WITH YOUR UNCLE, AFTER IT ALL happened. Uncle Glenn. Remember him? He did his best to look after you, those few days you were with him after the Bad Stuff, but he never wanted children, certainly didn't want his brother's daughter. It didn't fit into his lifestyle. He liked his drink and his darts. His nights out at the pub where he'd traipse back to his flat about two in the morning.

But he knew it was the right thing to do, after that night, taking you in. That's why he offered.

And you needed someone. Someone external. Someone who could see the pain in your eyes. And Uncle Glenn could. It haunted him.

But he knew he didn't know how to deal with you, what to say, what to do, how to help you cope.

He was so worried, because he didn't really know you Seeing you once a year at Christmas didn't mean anything. He didn't have anything to compare the new you to. And he did his best.

He found your sketch pads first. Those pages and pages filled with HURT HURT HURT. The word written over and over in different typographies—remember those? You spent hours on them. And then he saw your drawings. The insects and the eyes and the knives and the blades.

He'd seen that sketch pad with you a lot. You carried it everywhere.

But I digress.

You needed them, your parents, and they weren't there. Only Uncle Glenn was, and you can't blame him. You've been through a lot.

Your uncle read up on Abuse and Parenting and Trauma and Survivors and Grief, and he wanted to know you, to help you. You saw the books he'd got out of the library, the ones he tried to hide from you, but you knew he'd been in contact with Dr. Tim Everest, an old classmate of his who became a psychotherapist.

You insisted there was nothing wrong with you. That you were coping.

Because that's what the insects told you to say.

And it wasn't your uncle's fault.

You were up in the bathroom that evening. The evening when he later realized how little he knew you and how much he'd missed. When he realized the help you needed, the help you wrote all around you.

You stared at the black-and-white tiles for what felt like hours. Really, it was seven-and-a-half minutes. But the eyes that you saw everywhere were watching you. One in each tile. And then the eyes were stepping forward, and cartoon insects popped out of each square.

They ran down the walls to the bathtub, then across the taps, and down to the floor, scurried across the linoleum or whatever flooring you had, and up to you. They swarmed you.

You tried to get them off you.

I tried to get them off you, though I could not see them myself, only see them through your eyes.

You screamed that they were burrowing into you.

We both screamed as you used the razor blade to cut them out of your skin.

Bad Dream

A BAD DREAM. THAT'S ALL IT IS. A BAD DREAM.

An invention. To scare me.

I swallow hard.

You need to accept reality. You need help. I'm sorry I've…enabled all of this. I didn't realize you were still so bad. But you really need to go back to The De Hewitt Facility.

"No!" I scream.

Then I shake my head so hard my neck hurts. Not to the Offenders. Not to the Offenders. Not to the Offenders.

They're not Offenders there, Brooke.

"I'm not Brooke!"

You invented that. You made your own dystopian reality because you love those books. But you need to open your eyes, please.

No. No. No.

Come on, Brooke, you know he touched you. You remember.

Signs

IN MY ROOM, I EXAMINE MY FOREHEAD. I LOOK for signs of the branding scar, but there aren't any. I know I should feel pleased. That's good. Very good. No one can trace me to my Offender activity. To the man I killed (or didn't kill).

But pressing my hand flat against my forehead fills me with a strange sensation. The skin is smooth. Like milk. Like there was never anything there.

I try to sleep, but I can't. All I can think about is that damn rat.

I get out next week's university reading, ready to get ahead, but I can't concentrate on the words, can't take anything in. My mind is thinking on its own, independently, doing what it wants. And Chaos isn't even active now.

I roll over, pull my duvet around me tighter. Somehow, from here, I can hear the tap in the bathroom dripping.

It gets to quarter to two, and then I can't stand it. I get out of bed, pull my leather jacket on over my pajamas, find some shoes, and I leave the house.

It's a lot darker outside than I'd realized, and I should've brought a torch. Can barely see a few feet in front of me.

I get to the place where I left the rat's cage, and I see it there, its rectangular shape. I rush over, shaking from the cold.

"It's all right, Freddie," I say. "I'm sorry, I'm back now, and—"

The cage is empty.

Freddie's gone.

Anguish

I CRY AND CRY, AND EVERYTHING'S GOING wrong. The world is going wrong. It's being folded up, and I'm getting flattened between its pages.

And…

And Freddie. The rat. I need him back. I was wrong. He wasn't a spy. He was innocent. He was my responsibility, just like my sister was. I let her down, and I can't let him down.

I'm on my knees and hands, scrabbling about in the dirt.

———

I RETURN TO THE HOUSE ABOUT AN HOUR after dawn.

"Hey, what's the matter?" Bradley corners me the moment I get inside the house. His gym bag is in his hand, and he looks like he's on the way out.

"Nothing." I try to push away from him, but he stops me with a hand on my arm.

"Uh, your mother's here. I actually just yelled up the stairs for you."

"What?"

"She said it was a surprise—something about a tradition you both have for the last day of February?" He gives me an apologetic look. "I can stall her for a bit while you get cleaned up." He gestures to my face.

"Uh, yeah…"

"Is that her?" a woman's voice calls, and then there's footsteps and…

It's her. The woman from the Facebook account.

It's not my mother behind that account. It feels like a punch to the gut. Why isn't my mother in contact with me at all?

The fake mother stops and lets out a laugh. "Oh, I thought that was my Em getting home."

Bradley frowns. "This is Emilia."

The woman laughs. "This isn't my daughter."

"Emilia Johnson?" Bradley swivels slowly toward me, his whole body turning toward me, like he's a puppet.

"*I'm* Emilia Johnson," I say, but my voice is weak.

"This is not my daughter. Where's my daughter?"

My legs start to shake. My cover's been blown.

Oh God.

I run.

Kira

I RUN TO RAVEN'S HOUSE. I TELL HIM THAT MY cover's been blown or that I'm going mad. I don't know which it is. He watches me for a long time. Then we kiss.

Stupid Little Girl

YOU REALLY ARE STUPID, AREN'T YOU? A STUPID little girl. So deluded—thinking you can get your fairy-tale ending with Raven! Well, I've got news for you, girl.

Wake up! For God's sake. None of this is real!

Are you really not talking to me?

Going to sulk? Pretend pretend pretend?

Well, I've had enough.

You think you deserve to have a body?

Well. You don't. It's mine now.

If I can't get out of your body, Brooke, then you're getting out of it. Because I don't want to share anymore.

Kira vs Chaos

"JUST STOP! FOR GOD'S SAKE, STOP! WE NEED to sort this—my cover's been blown!"

No! You were never supposed to be Emilia Johnson. No one told you to be her, Brooke.

"No, they did!"

No. That was you. I'll tell you what happened. I'll tell you all the stuff that you conveniently forgot so you could live a more exciting life.

"Just stop! Stop trying to distract me!"

Here, sit comfortably, won't you?

Let's Go Back a Bit

THEY'D BOOKED THE HOSPITAL TRANSPORT FOR one o'clock. You didn't want to leave The Facility. You didn't want to leave your friends. You and Maria were crying and hugging, and Jase and Gaz were standing farther back, looking awkward and out of place.

Monika was there to see you off. She wasn't going to be traveling with you, but Raymond was, along with the driver.

"It's been wonderful getting to know you," Monika said to you, and she shook your hand. This surprised you, and you stared at her for a few moments, noticing the emerging breakout on her chin. You decided shaking hands was definitely preferable to a hug as you didn't want to get too close.

"You have The Facility's details," Monika said, chirpy. You wondered if she was pleased you were going. You weren't her favorite. Definitely not the easiest. "You can contact us—and your friends—if you want to or need to. Phone calls are at seven, remember."

She gave you a big smile.

Maria started crying all over again.

And then you got into the van. The ambulance van.

Raymond got in next to you, carrying a briefcase that contained your case notes. He was making the journey with you, and you weren't pleased. Neither was he. He didn't say it, but you could tell by the glassy look in his eyes and the way he sighed.

You stared at The Facility out of the window, until it disappeared from sight. You felt empty, like you hadn't eaten the sandwich they'd insisted you eat. You couldn't even feel the chewed-up bread and cheese churning around in the slush in your stomach. There was nothing there that you could feel.

"I want to go back," you whispered, and you tried to keep your voice level and calm. You didn't want it to wobble.

"You'll be fine," Raymond said. "You'll be closer to your uncle—and North Devon District Hospital has a great program. Plus, they do intensive out-patient treatments in Barnstaple, too, so if all goes well in your stay, they may let you live at home after *a while, if you improve. And that's what we want. We want to get you back out there. We want you better."*

We want you better.

Those words rang over and over in your head for the next hour or so. The van then stopped at a service station, and Raymond bought you some herbal tea and the driver went to the other end of the car park to smoke.

After twenty minutes, you all got back in. You couldn't see the driver because of the partition behind him, but you know he turned the key because the van rumbled to life.

Then the engine stuttered. Something made a clanky noise, then the strong smell of burning filled your nostrils.

You all got out of the van.

It was suddenly a lot more crowded in the car park for the service station now, and a coach had pulled up next to you. What seemed to you like hundreds of older teenagers leapt off the coach and started yelling and moaning and complaining.

Nearby, you could see Raymond and the driver looking at the ambulance's engine or something. The teenagers around you got even louder.

You covered your ears as you looked around.

Over there. There was a safe place over there.

By a tree.

You walked over to it. The air felt cleaner, like there was less competition for the oxygen. You breathed deeper, and you tried to remember the coping techniques that Matt had taught you, what you should do when you start feeling overwhelmed and scared.

But you couldn't remember.

And then there was another coach, and lots and lots of people were getting on that, and somehow you ended up on it, too. You were scared—your heart was beating fast—and you looked out the window and saw Raymond and the driver and the van. The two of them were looking at a booklet or something, while the driver had his phone to his ear. You pressed your hands to the window as the coach drove past them.

Your body suddenly jolted, and you knew you had to get off. Your hands trembled as you stood up and—

"Sit down!" a man yelled. "Seat belt on!"

You sat down quickly, and you put your seat belt on.

You had a double-seat to yourself, so you looked across the aisle for someone who could help you. There was a couple in their mid-forties on the other side and you saw they were wearing brightly colored shirts with palm trees on and beige shorts and sandals.

Your mouth got a little drier.

At this point, I told you to shout, and I tried to forcibly take over your body and actions rather than just be here, aware for the later narration, but I couldn't—who knows, maybe I was just too tired—I had spent a long time being in control when I got you out of The Facility. I couldn't take over you, I couldn't help you, and you weren't listening to my instructions.

You stayed on the bus until it got to Exeter bus station, the coach's destination. You waited until most people had got off the bus and you were surprised no one checked your papers or anything—not that you had them—and then you were standing in the bus station you didn't really know. Because although your uncle lived in North Devon, your family home had been in Bristol.

You looked around. You tried to work out what to do.

You felt sick. The weak kind of shaky sick. Not the actual vomit sick.

You walked to the covered seats, at the back of the bus station, through a little partition doorway. There was one man there with beautiful dark skin and nice arms. You *thought about going to ask him for help, but you didn't know what you'd say, and you knew you shouldn't talk to strangers.*

You walked to the back row of seats. It was cold under the covered area, but you were starting to sweat.

Then you saw a bag on the seat farthest to the left. You looked back toward the man, but he was looking at his phone screen. Something told you it wasn't his bag.

You took the bag, and you went out and down some steps and into a bathroom and you looked through its contents. A phone. A purse. A laptop. Two shirts, a hoodie, a hat, some underwear, purple tights, a skirt, and some heels.

You discovered the clothes were your size and you put a new outfit on. Then you opened the small purse at the bottom of the bag, with the driver's license and the University ID card in it. You said the name several times.

"Emilia Johnson."

You decided to become Emilia Johnson, and you begged me to tell you a story about how this girl was to be your new identity, to protect you from people who know that you're Untrustworthy, but I wouldn't do that. So, you told the story yourself, and you believed it.

I told you to go to the office at the station to get help, to contact The Facility.

But you wouldn't listen to me. I even told you to do it for the next few days, but it was like you couldn't even hear those words. You only heard me say what you wanted, then, because you responded to other stuff I said, but not that. I figured there was nothing I could do. So, I had to go along with it. With you being Emilia. Had to help you keep her identity. Did you know I was even messaging regularly with Emilia's mother? Trying to stop her getting worried? I even looked back at their previous correspondence so I could get the tone just right.

And I was jealous, I'll admit it. You got a fresh start—but I didn't. I was still trapped in you, part of you that could never escape.

It was just luck that when you were standing back in the bus station forecourt, Emilia's phone rang and it was her new flat mates who she'd not yet met. And then you met the housemates and they had no reason to suspect you weren't Emilia. After all, you even had the bag that Emilia has with her in her Facebook profile photo (as Beth had been stalking Emilia's social media to make sure she wasn't inviting some weirdo into her house--now isn't that funny?) and your hair had been freshly dyed black because that was something I asked to be done at The Facility. I told them you wanted a new life—new hair, new start, all of that—and Monika was actually quite pleased. She had a nurse help you do it. Of course, I didn't know then that Emilia was a Goth or that your faces kind of look similar—although I know a lot, I didn't predict that—but it all just fell into place.

You were ecstatic. Slipping into her life like that was great. You couldn't have planned it better yourself.

But what about poor Emilia? You've never even thought about her because you've erased the truth from your mind.

Don't you care about her? Don't you want to know what happened that meant she left her bag—with her most prized possessions—on a seat in the bus station?

Well, lucky for you, I have found out.

She was taken.

And if you had raised the alarm when you found her bag, and if police had taken prints from that bag, well, then she wouldn't now be dead.

Identity

MY NOSE IS RUNNING, BUT I HAVEN'T GOT A tissue. It runs everywhere.

And if you had raised the alarm when you found her bag, and if police had taken prints from that bag, well, then she wouldn't now be dead.

I don't know whether Chaos says the words again or whether I just hear them again.

I swallow hard, staring at the wall in front of me. The pristine white tiles. I don't recognize them, but that doesn't even seem significant. Because all I can concentrate on are those words. And what they mean.

My fault.

My fault.

I took Emilia's identity by accident?

I stare at the wall. It can't be right. Can't be true.

Chaos is lying.

I'm not lying. Why would I lie? This is exhausting being in your head. It's horrible. I want you to get better and to get me out. You need help. And you've come off all your medication so suddenly and look what it's doing. They can help you. Just tell someone who you are, Brooke. Tell them you're Brooke Taylor. They're looking for you.

I stiffen. Why can't Chaos do that, control me, and tell them who I am? She controlled me before.

I don't know why. I can't do it now. And I should've told someone when I pretended to be you and got you with Josh and all that after we argued—but I just wanted some fun. I wanted to be me, just for a moment.

I'm sorry.

I grab onto the kitchen counter suddenly, and I look up. In the window, I see Emilia's face.

I scream and then Raven's in the kitchen. Raven—he's really here? This place… I blink hard, pain lingering behind my eyes.

"What is it?" he asks, but it's just my face in the window now.

Just me. Short, dirty blond hair and a reddened face from crying too much.

"Nothing."

I rush past him, trying to work out where we are, where to go—but I end up ascending the stairs. We're not in the summer house anymore. It's a proper house. A good house. A house that says it will protect me—and I feel it, feel this house whispering to me. Telling me to turn left on the landing, into an empty room that's got a mattress on.

My room. This is my safe place now. I've been here before—earlier today? Or was it yesterday? Did I sleep on this mattress last night?

Oh, Brooke. You really need help.

I throw myself down on the mattress and imagine all sorts of nasty bugs crawling out from it onto me, and then they're consuming me, and I can see their eyes. Those big cartoon eyes.

I curl up, and I cry.

Friends

TWO OF RAVEN'S FRIENDS COME ROUND A FEW hours later. Donna and Alexandra. They're both mid-twenties, I'd say, and they smile at each other in the kitchen, not *to* each other. Like they're performing or something. Their smiles aren't genuine, and I am confused.

I left my mattress a little while ago, feeling strangely comforted by the house, yet not understanding everything altogether.

"Yep. We'll move in here," Alexandra says, flicking her braids over her shoulder.

"Hundred a week?" Raven says. And just as Alexandra and Donna groan, he says, "Come on. *I* found the house. And I had to pay *you* for the summerhouse. Time for me to be landlord now."

The women nod.

"Fine," Alexandra says.

"Perfect," Donna says.

Perfect.

I want to be PERFECT.

I want to look down and see it written on my arm. But written permanently, like Raven's tattoos. The tattoos he has on his biceps. The dark swirls.

Or are they just in the stories? I frown, and I don't know. But I need a tattoo.

"Where can I get a tattoo?" I ask.

Raven's eyebrows shoot up. "I can do it."

"You can?"

He looks back at his friends, and they share a look. Something passes through the air that I don't quite understand.

"You'll have to decide what you want," Donna says.

"The U," I say, and I point to my forehead, because it needs to be there. Back where it belongs.

"What?" Raven frowns. So do Donna and Alexandra. Too many frowns, frowning at me.

"U for Untrustworthy," I say. Are they really going to pretend like they don't know?

The corners of Donna's mouth lift up. Alexandra widens her eyes at Raven. Raven doesn't say a word.

"Well, you'll have to design it," Donna says. "The font and everything that you want for this…U. Because Raven's got no imagination himself."

"It doesn't take a lot of imagination," I say. "It's the U."

"Come on, I've got books of designs upstairs," Raven says. "You can choose now or you can draw it."

"Now?" I blink.

"No time like the present."

I follow him up the stairs.

"She's crazy," I hear Donna say, and she thinks I can't hear her, but her words chase me.

"Here are the books." Raven hands me two thin paperbacks, because suddenly we're upstairs. "Flip through them and find a font you like."

Okay. That's easy enough.

I sit in the chair in the corner of the room, by the window. There are dead bluebottles on the windowsill. They're all lying upside down. Raven's steps are heavy as he heads back downstairs. I hear the murmur of his voice with the others'. They're talking. About me. I just know it.

But it's just a test. The game-makers are trying to see how paranoid I am.

It'll be okay.

It'll be fine.

I thumb through the pages. So many words. Words I want to cut out and put on my skin, etch them onto me forever.

I like words a lot. "Did I tell you that?"

You told me.

"You sound annoyed."

I'm not annoyed. Just fed-up. Bored. I mean, you can't actually stay in this crack house.

"It's not a crack house. It's Raven's home."

If you say so.

Chaos's tone is annoying me, so I block her out. It's like reaching inside of me and putting my hand around her throat and squeezing as hard as I can, until she can't make a sound. Until she is lifeless…dead.

No. Not dead.

She can't die.

She can only be resurrected.

"Resurrected." I like the way the word flows. Maybe that should be my tattoo. Maybe I don't want the U. But which one would get me a better score? More points in this game? Because this has to be a game.

I look out the window. Not much of a view. A brick wall, looking shabby, with some concrete blocks stacked against it.

I look back down at the dead bluebottles. They're no longer upside down.

I frown.

"Glitch," I mutter, smiling.

"Oh my God," Donna says from downstairs. Her tone is high and full of alarm, and it is like a little dagger that digs into my spine. That forces me to stand up.

I head downstairs.

"Do you see this?" Donna is waving her mobile phone at Raven and Alexandra. There's a news article on it.

"What is it?" I ask.

The three of them jump when they see me.

"They've just found a body," Donna says. "A woman called Emilia Johnson."

The Real Girl

A BODY. A BODY. A BODY.

Emilia Johnson. The real Emilia Johnson.

I feel sick.

My fault. Chaos was right. I found her things, and I should've reported it. And—and someone's killed her.

Killed Emilia Johnson.

Killed me.

No. Not me. I'm not her.

Oh, God.

My body feels like it's going to explode.

She's dead.

I should be dead.

No.

And then my fingers are itching for the only thing that can make it right. But I haven't got the blade here.

So, I root through the drawers in the kitchen, but all the cutlery's gone and the knife block is empty. I pull out more drawers and boxes full of rubbish.

At last, I find a pin.

It's a sewing pin. A tiny thing, bent.

But it's sharp. Very sharp.

Stop it.

I look around. Raven's not here. No one is. Where'd he and the others go? Vaguely, I remember him saying something about food. Or did I imagine that? I don't know. I look at the clock. It's late. How can it be so late?

But the time doesn't matter.

Just the pin.

And then—then I find a needle at the back of the drawer.

A needle that is sharper and bigger and better.

Divided

YOU'RE BLEEDING, AND IT'S GOING EVERYWHERE.

I don't know what to do.

I scream at you, tell you to stop, but you don't listen. You don't listen at all. It's like you can't hear me, like before. Maybe you can't hear me. There's no acknowledgment. You don't hear anything. There's a wall between us, and it's getting bigger, a divide. Something to stop me talking to you. Something to stop me talking to my only friend.

And you are my friend.

So, I do it again, because no matter what you think, I do love you. How can I not love you when I've been with you for so long? And it's easier now, taking control of you, suddenly so easy and—

I feel the pain, and it's gushing gushing gushing.

Emilia's phone is in the pocket of your jeans on the foldup chair. I make you get up, and I make you get your phone. You blood spills everywhere.

I ignore all the missed calls from Beth and Bradley and Cassie and Emilia's mother, just scroll through your contacts. You already added Raven to Emilia's phone.

I call Raven.

"Help me," I say, in your voice, and I'm trying to help you, but...

But it's getting so dark... and...and where are you going, Brooke? Where are you—

Brooke?

"BROOKE? HEY—OH FUCK. BROOKE?"

The voice is echoey and strange, and it feels like it's got little hands that are holding onto me in all the places I don't want to be held onto and then it's…

My eyes flutter open. Two eyes stare back at me.

"Raven?"

He's breathing hard, and he's trying to wrap something around my arm.

My arm?

I blink slowly, and then I see the redness. The blood.

My stomach twists sharply, and I see dark spots around me.

"Where's your phone?" Raven's looking at me.

My phone? I frown. No…no phone.

"I need to call an ambulance—your phone? Mine was nearly out when you phoned, and I can't find the charger and—"

"No! No ambulance… No, Raven…"

He shakes his head. And then I realize that I'm naked, and I'm sprawled out across his lap, and he's shirtless, and my face is against the hard planes of his chest.

Life thuds into me, and I push myself away from him. My hands flail out for something, anything to cover me, and—

"Keep your arm up, we've got to stop the bleeding," Raven says.

I look back at him. He's kneeling in blood.

So much blood.

My blood.

Oh God.

Persuasion

I PERSUADE HIM NOT TO CALL AN AMBULANCE, and he agrees. I try to tell him that if I go to the hospital, I'll get caught. Everyone's looking for Brooke Taylor—because Barry Norman's escaped and because one of my housemates will have gone to the police about me and they'll have worked out who I am—and now I'll be implicated in the murder of the real Emilia Johnson, and it's all such a mess.

Raven sterilizes my cuts as best as he can and uses the little money he has to buy more first aid stuff. When he goes out to the shops to get it, he calls one of his friends, and a woman named Flower comes to watch me. Not Donna or Alexandra or Dilly. Flower isn't happy about it but says she used to be a cutter too, so she knows what it feels like. Then she does this whole pep talk, spitting out what her therapist said to her.

By the time Raven's back, Flower seems to think she's fixed me.

I just let her think that. How can a twenty-minute conversation with a woman I don't know and don't like 'fix' me?

And what if I can't be fixed? Or I don't need to be. Why must perfect people be only happy?

What if I can never be happy because I'm Untrustworthy?

No, you can be happy. You will be.

A label doesn't define you.

DONNA IS BACK, AND SHE WANTS MY OPINION on her next haircut. She shows me a photo of a girl with short hair on her phone. "What do you think, chick?"

Chick. Chick. Chick. I mouth the word, and think of…no, I can't remember her name. So I take the phone from Donna and stare at the screen, then look around the room. We're in a different room. A room with a desk, and lots of things on the desk. Pens and pencils and papers and books.

Down below, I hear a knock on the door, then the sounds of Raven stomping across the kitchen and out to the hall, presumably to answer it.

I peer at the phone, at the girl who looks pretty androgynous but has a cool spiky hairdo. Somewhere, there's a memory of Raven with the same spiky hairstyle, but I can't quite place it.

That's because it didn't happen. It was what you wanted me to make up—that date with him. A story to comfort you. See? This is what happens when you get me to tell you stories but then I also have to tell you the truth of what's going on—you get mixed up, you don't know what's fact and what's fiction anymore. It's only natural and—

"Get out!" Raven shouts suddenly. "Get out!"

And then there's another voice and—

Oh, God.

That voice.

My heart pounds, I let out a small squeak. My hands go clammy.

Donna looks up at me, her brow furrowed. She starts toward the door, her new haircut forgotten.

There's a crash downstairs.

And more movement, and then I'm losing time, and my head's hurting, and I'm thinking about waspkeepers. And what the hell are waspkeepers?

My phone buzzes. It's a new phone. One I don't recognize at first—but didn't Raven get this for me? Was it yesterday? Was there a whole day between the razors and Donna coming back? I don't know, but I told Raven I couldn't use Emilia's anymore, didn't I?

Wait—how much time has passed?

I frown, pick up the phone, stare at the screen.

The text is from Raven: *Get out. Norman is here.*

Cue: Panic

AT FIRST YOU FEEL LIKE YOU CAN'T BREATHE. *You mutter to yourself that this can't be real. You breathe heavily and turn, knocking something off the desk. A tattoo book. You freeze and stare at it though. Then you hear bad sounds downstairs. And it's him. You know it.*

I know it.

You go cold. But your insides feel like they're melting. You grab your pen from the desk, where you put it earlier. You write HELP *on the back of your right hand, and you show it to Donna.*

Then you go into survival mode.

You have to get out, you know that.

Laughter comes from downstairs.

He's laughing at you.

He knows you're there. You can hear Raven shouting again. And then there's another crashing sound. Someone grunts.

"Who is it?" Donna whispers, and she's grabbing a baseball bat from behind the door. You didn't know it was there.

You stare at her, but you can't say his name.

She doesn't wait for your answer. She heads downstairs.

You look around, your heart pounding. You're sweating. You're drenched in stale sweat. The HELP you wrote is blurring.

You can tell from their voices that they're downstairs, directly beneath you. You can't go down there to escape from the back door or the front door because they're there. Raven and Donna and Mr. Norman.

The window. You stare at it. It's your only option.

Run. Run. Run.

You race toward it and slam your phone to your thigh so hard it'll bruise later. You squish it in your pocket then you climb up onto the desk and struggle with the window catch. You curse under your breath.

The landing outside your door creaks. You inhale sharply.

You freeze. A second. Two seconds.

It's just the house talking to you. Telling you to get out. Don't be scared—please don't be scared.

You turn back to the window and at last you manage to open it. Cold air rushes in, and its fingers pull you out.

You're one floor up, but you slide down onto the porch roof and you drop onto the pavement gracefully. You crouch on the ground. You're below the living room window. Barry Norman is inside…

RUN.

Running

HE FOLLOWED ME, THAT ONE TIME I RAN OUT, left the house before he gave me permission. Maybe a year ago. Of course he followed me. And I never was quick at running. Two minutes, and I was out of breath. I flicked my head around, and he was right behind me, screaming and cursing.

My heart pounded as I forced myself to run faster. I had to. No choice. If I could just get away from these lanes and out into the roads where there were houses… And it was a sunny day so there'd have to be someone gardening or mowing the lawn or something. Someone who could help.

But the U on my forehead burned.

And then his hand landed on my shoulder, and he was on me. I fell heavily to the ground, and his weight trapped me.

His smell—lager and chalk—clogged my nostrils. I tried to get away, to get out from under his body.

But I couldn't. Of course I couldn't.

"You're going to behave now, aren't you?" His voice was gruff. Full of danger. One of his hands slid under my chest, and then he squeezed my left breast, painfully. "You're *going* to behave."

I nodded. There was nothing else I could do. Tears came to my eyes.

"Good."

With that, he hauled me up. I looked around quickly. I needed a weapon—something—but there was nothing. His hand remained on my shoulder.

"Come on." Mr. Norman pulled me along.

The walk back to the prison seemed to take ages. He smiled at me the whole way. Didn't speak. There was no talk of what he was going to do to me. No dark promise. Just that smile. A smile that stretched on and on, and the future baby's cry that only I could hear.

"No one will ever believe you! Your word against mine. I think we both know who will win."

I Spy With My Little Eye...
the Present Day

I NEED TO FIND MY PARENTS. I HAVE TO GO to them.

You can't go and find your parents. You just can't. It's better if you don't. Better for you. I don't want you to find out like this.

But Chaos is wrong. Chaos doesn't know me. Chaos is an intruder. And she's dangerous.

So I run, and I find a bus stop with a timetable on it, and I use the only coins I have on me to get as near to Bristol as I can. It takes a couple of hours, but then I'm in Bristol, and I'm walking down a road that I think is the right road, and everywhere I look, I see the posters for me. My face plasters the street. Because they know an Untrustworthy is on the run and she's not in a Lowers' area, and I'm bad.

People die and—

You can't go to your house!

Chaos suddenly shouts at me, and I think she's been shouting all the time, screaming at me, but somehow, I tuned it out. Her shouts became the rumble of the bus's engine and the grunt-grunt-grunt of the old man's breath and the barking of a small dog that I think trotted past me on the pavement at some point with two middle-aged women and a younger man.

And then I'm in front of my house, and I stare at it, stare at the boarded-up windows. And the 'For Sale' sign in the garden. My parents are moving, and they didn't tell me? They never even visited me at The Facility…and they're just trying to vanish…without me. Without their daughter who's a disappointment. An Offender. An Untrustworthy.

Just listen, will you! It's gone too far, this game, this pretense! You need to—

But I don't listen, because why would I listen to her, this person inside me who changes so much, when I'm outside my parents' house and though the windows are boarded, I'm sure they're in there. Mum will be in the living room, reading one of the novels she likes to relax after a hard day of surgeries, and Dad will be on his computer. The TV will be on in the background.

I listen for the TV; I think I can hear it.

Then I'm rushing to the front door, and I'm pounding on it so much my fists hurt.

"There's no one there, love."

I turn to find a woman and a toddler behind me. They're wearing matching raincoats.

"What?" I say.

And Chaos inside me tries to speak, tries to be heard— but I won't let her.

The woman looks at me sideways. "The house has been empty since December. Estate agent says no interest in it, either. Not when the previous occupants were murdered in it."

A strange whirring sound fills my ears. My heart speeds up.

"Murdered?"

"Aye," the woman says. "By Barry Norman. He killed the parents. Only two survivors."

The Very Bad Stuff

"IF YOU SO MUCH AS TOUCH MY DAUGHTER again, I'll kill you."

Your dad's hand shook as he raised it up, as he pointed at Mr. Norman. He was trying to sound brave, you could tell that. But he didn't look brave. He looked terrified.

Your mother wasn't much better. She was trembling, and you wanted to go over to her. To both of them. But Mr. Norman's hand was on your shoulder, and you knew better than to move when he was touching you.

You wished your parents hadn't come. You knew how it would end—deep down, you knew, even though part of you still pretended you didn't. Even then, without me helping you, interacting, you were intuitive. You felt things. And you felt the looming presence of the Bad Stuff.

"I'm the one with the gun. Yet you're the one making threats," Mr. Norman said slowly, his eyes drifting over to you and then back to your parents. "I'd be very careful if I were you."

"The cops are coming!" your dad yelled. "They know what you've been doing to my daughter and you're not getting away with it anymore."

"Stupid man." Mr. Norman lifted the gun and fired once, twice, three times.

You screamed.

My Parents Are Dead

TWO SURVIVORS.

Two.

"Are you all right?" The woman with the toddler is staring at me.

I stare back at her, as if the staring is a competition. I take in her bright red lipstick that doesn't go with the rest of her outfit. Her worn-out tracksuit top covered in stains and the leggings that are losing their elasticity. Her child starts mumbling and gurgling. Their matching raincoats have gone. Disappeared.

"Mummy! I want to go *nooooow!*" And then the little boy's face is pinching up and he's pointing at me and saying, "Bad woman bad woman bad woman."

Bad woman bad woman bad woman.

I look down at my hand, at *BAD*. I take out a pen from behind my ear and add WOMAN underneath. But then the letters of WOMAN rearrange and change a little and become NORMAN, and I scream.

"Are you—"

I turn and run, skid on something wet and slimy on the short grass, and nearly fall. The world whips around behind me, and then it's closing in, chasing me. And it's squeezing, squeezing like it's a birth canal and I'm the baby and it's trying to deliver me, pull me out of this darkness and into a new kind where the Bad Stuff will happen all over again.

And NORMAN is on my hand, he's here. I can't get away from him.

I blanch as I hear gunshots.

Just your mind. Told you that you were mad. Chaos shouts the words, and then I realize I've dropped the pen, and I turn but I can't stop, and my feet hit each other, and there's pain and—

Dead. Dead. Dead.

My parents are dead.

My gut squeezes.

But someone survived. Two. The woman said two. Survivors always come in pairs. Me and Chaos. She's the second person. She has to be. She's my sister: Brooke, Bringer of Chaos. That's why people have been calling me her name, mixing us up. Is Brooke still alive?

I smell my father's aftershave in the wind, and then the sky's painted with the floral design of my mother's favorite skirt. The one she wore at the funeral. The funeral I didn't go to. The funeral Chaos told me about.

But Chaos lied.

Not my abuser's funeral. My *parents'* funeral.

And then—then I see them.

They're lying still, and I'm looking down at them—yet I'm running at the same time—and they're in the boxes, and my mother's face is heavily made up in garish colors that she'd never wear. She never wore makeup because the sun shone through her eyes, and she didn't need more beauty and—

Bad woman bad woman bad woman.

Me. BAD. Me. SO BAD.

Because I told them. Told my parents, the only people I've ever belonged to, and then Mr. Norman killed them. Their deaths: my fault.

I thought I could stop the murders… I thought that by exposing him, I'd stop them. Stop the deaths.

But it didn't work.

I suck in air too quickly, feel something in my chest spasm. A horn suddenly blares, and I look up and a car hurtles toward me.

I run faster. Got to get away, got to—

Someone screams.

Not me.

Tires squeal.

Someone is laughing. *Ha ha ha.*

My body smacks into someone, and then his hands rush out and grab me.

I look up to see and—

Mr. Norman smiles down at me. "I told you that you'd never be alone."

Smells Like Smoke

EVERYTHING STOPS.

Your body locks up.

You think it's him. Unmistakably him. That's all you can think. You're just thinking that it's him, and you don't even take in what happens, what this man is doing.

I fight to take over, to get control of your body—you can't go with him. But you're stronger now. Shit. And I can't take control again. I'm trapped, trapped in your body, a helpless bystander.

His car is parked around the corner, and he takes you to it. You get in as he guides you in. You don't protest. There's a CCTV camera pointing this way down the street, and it will look like you're a willing participant in this whole...whatever it is. Because it's not kidnapping. Not when you willingly get in, when you don't fight him.

The inside of his car smells like smoke. You sit in the passenger seat, and you don't notice when he puts the child locks on—but I do. You just stare straight ahead. I want you to look around, so I can see the details, anything that might come in handy, but you don't.

It starts to rain.

He doesn't say a word to you. Or to himself. He just keeps his eyes on the road and his hands tightly around the steering wheel so that his knuckles are white. He's applying a lot of pressure. Maybe he'll apply that amount of pressure to your neck. Then where will we be? Because I could fight him, but you've locked me out from controlling us. And you're not going to fight him.

Think, think of something!

Okay. I need to remain calm. I can work out what's around us, even if you don't look around. I let my senses free, let them wander.

There's a mobile phone under your seat. You don't know it's there, but I do. I want to make you reach down and get it, make you send a text to someone.

Oh, please, let me help you.

You smile and turn to the man.

"So what's your name?" he asks, and that should be your first clue, but I know you don't hear that question. You hear something different, and you let out a yelp.

"No need to be shy," he says. "You want a drink? Loosen you up? There's a six-pack of beer in the back. You can reach it."

He's looking at you, but you don't register his words, because all you heard when he spoke was "I was always going to find you again."

A humming sensation fills your head, and—shit. You're flashbacking. You're not even present as the man puts his hand on your knee.

You're folding inside yourself, remembering those distorted days.

And I'm still trapped, caged inside of you, as this complete stranger drives us away.

The Body On the Final Night of the Bad Stuff

SHE WAS BROKEN. LYING THERE, BROKEN. Blond hair splayed out and—

"What do you think you're doing?" came a voice from behind me.

I screamed and ran, and somehow, I got past him, through the doorway. I scrambled up the stairs, into the hallway and—

I grabbed the potted plant from the table beside me. The pot was heavy, ceramic, and I hit Mr. Norman over the head with it. Don't know how I did it. But I did.

And he fell back, and it gave me the time I needed.

My heart pounded as I ran through the house, as I got to the door, as I rattled the handle, as I begged the lock to give. But it didn't. I felt sick as I looked back, as I saw Mr. Norman stirring on the floor. And there was blood. Blood from his head.

Get out. Get out. Get out! Chaos screamed, and she was right. I needed to get out. I turned and ran. The living room. The window. I knew it opened wide.

It was already open a few inches. I pushed the pane back the rest of the way, looked behind me—Mr. Norman still hadn't appeared, but I could hear him groaning. I pulled myself up onto the window frame, caught my shin on something and grimaced. Cold air held onto my body, pulled me outside. And then I lost my balance or something because I crashed down onto the hard ground sooner than I expected and—

And I was outside.

For several moments, I crouched below the window, breathing hard, my eyes glassing over. I was outside. Outside. Outside. Free.

Run.

Run.

I ran. Sweat poured down me, down my back, drenching my shirt. My arms pumped frantically at my sides. I felt the first lingers of lactic acid burning into my thighs, and the lactic acid had a haughty face, but it was laughing with me because I was going to expose him, and we both wanted him exposed. I was going to stop him hurting me, stop him hurting other girls and boys.

And I could do it. I knew I could.

I kept on running, lungs inhaling the winter air. My bare feet slapped the pavement, and I was emitting a strange high-pitched noise as I ran because suddenly, every time I blinked I saw the dead girl's marred body. And there was blood on my hands, like a layer of PVA glue sticking to me.

I looked up, left or right. My house or the police station?

The junction got nearer, and I still didn't know which way to go.

My house or the police station?

But I had to. Had to make a decision.

I turned left, and that was when the Bad Stuff started, because that's when I led him to my parents.

Run!

KIRA! KIRA, NOW REALLY ISN'T THE TIME TO think about all that—

"Almost there, babe," the man says. His hand squeezes your thigh again. Even through your jeans, his fingers are searing.

I try to fight him, try to break my way into your body, but I can't. You've put too many barriers up and—

The man pulls his car into a driveway. The house is at the side of the road. Peeling gray paint. Rubbish in the overgrown garden.

"We'll have some fun now," he tells you.

And you're oblivious, staring down at your hands. UNTRUSTWORTHY.

Let me in! Give me control, don't block me out.

But you're not listening.

You're just…gone.

And the man's opening your door now, peeling you out of the car. And for the first time, I feel fear. My own fear. Fear for both of us.

After the Very Bad Stuff

"HEY, HEY, IT'S OKAY. IT'S OKAY."

The woman kept saying that. But it wasn't okay. It couldn't ever be okay. Not when my mum…my dad…

Tears slid down my face, and the *thing* upstairs was screaming.

"Get her away from here, Jane," a male voice said.

Away…

Away…

No, I couldn't leave my parents, couldn't….

But I blinked and I saw them—lying broken, like…*wrong* figures, bathed in red.

I screamed.

And I didn't think I could ever stop screaming.

A Stained Coffee Mug

HOT LIPS ON YOUR NECK, YOUR JAW. BURNING hands pulling at your clothes. You are rigid, unmoving, unresponsive. On the bed, and it's the same.

Come on!

I am screaming at you, but without you listening, I have no voice.

I am wordless.

You've got your words on your skin.

I have nothing. Not even a canvas to fill with messy writing and hopes and dreams and memories.

But I'll be the only one who remembers this. Everything that happens as I stare at the stained coffee mug on the windowsill.

WAKE UP, BROOKE!

Awake

I JOLT, FREEZE. HANDS ON ME. THE STENCH of sweat.

Mr. Norman—

No.

It's okay, I've got you. Just let me in.

It'll Be Okay Now

MY SOUL-BODY CLICKS INTO PLACE INSIDE yours. A skin burrowing inside a skin, and power floods me. Your body feels like mine—the only time when I feel like what I used to be again, a person.

And I have your body. I have you. My actions are yours, and I am programming you.

We're going to get out of here.

We shove the man back, and we're strong, my strength with yours. He staggers back, catches his back on the edge of the windowsill, and we spring up.

"What the fuck?" His eyes darken, and the way he's looking at us would scare you, but not me. Because I've seen this before— my own life, years and years ago. The man who hurt me killed me.

And maybe that's why I have drifted ever since, from girl to girl. Because we're the same, and like always calls to like. I know now not to humor you, play with you, annoy you, no matter how angry and broken I feel, because we are the same. I'm sorry, Brooke. So Sorry. But we're all we have. We have to stick together, because we are the girls people think they can hurt.

"I have to go." We spring toward the door, but he is quick, grabs us.

Our eyes widen. "Really? You're going to hold me here against my will?" We smile at him, and it is my favorite smile. The one that touches every part of me, and I've never felt this connected to you. To this all.

Before the man can reply, we punch him. A swift strike, just under the jaw. That fleshy, vulnerable place.

He screams, a guttural sound that grates on our ears. But he lets go of our arm.

We're turning, moving, and we're at the door. We yank it open, blinking. A hallway. We're upstairs. Dingy corridors, paint peeling. Cigarettes taint the air.

We surge forward, to the stairs—damp and dark, curtains are closed somewhere. Or just the doors to the other rooms, we can't tell. We're too focused on getting us out.

We've lost our shoes, and the carpet is hard and rough beneath our feet. Our heel lands in something sticky. We keep going. See the front door once we're at the bottom. Golden light pouring through the oval window in the door.

"Get back here!" the man yells. He's at the top of the stairs, taking them two at a time and—

Our hand is on the door. We yank it open.

And we run.

And we keep running.

And we are crying, and I feel you separating now from me, seeping back, trying to take over, but I've got to get us far away.

Far, far away.

"Are you okay?" a voice asks. A middle-aged woman that we run past. I see her only for a fraction of a second.

Street signs and houses and—

I know where we are. And it shouldn't be, because it can't be. We're not in Westward Ho! because we're in Bristol. We were literally by your house, before. Did… did that creep really drive us all the way out here?

I falter. It looks the same.

It all looks the same, and the world isn't right. Because roads lead to roads that they shouldn't, and we're running so fast, and trees are flying and—

And we are not well.

But it's okay. We're going to get better.

Uncle Glenn is Here

IT'S... I FROWN. A HOUSE. IT'S A HOUSE. AND I recognize it, but my mind is blurry, dark, and I can't remember. I need to put a light on and—

Knock on the door.

I go and knock on the door, and I think Chaos might still be controlling me because I feel like a robot. Not as much as I did before, as we traveled here, but…but not quite myself.

The door opens.

"Brooke?" A man with a paunchy belly and long, graying hair that's been gelled over to one side of his remarkably thin head stares at me. He's got a tea-towel or something draped over the shoulder of his purple, cotton shirt. A shirt that I recognize.

Uncle Glenn? I stare at him, feel a lump form in my throat.

It'll be okay now.

Then I jolt. "I'm not Brooke. I'm Kira." Does he really not know me?

"Where've you been?" He wraps me in a hug, and he seems different. Thinner—like I remember hugging him before, a comparison that easily finds me. "Come in, come in."

He ushers me into the living room. There are empty pizza boxes everywhere, and he hurriedly moves them, gestures for me to sit on the sofa. Where there's a baby's pacifier. It's a soft pink. A baby monitor sits on the mantelpiece opposite. A highchair stands before the table on the other side of the room, watching.

I sit on the sofa, feeling strange, like I'm going to sink and keep sinking until I've been swallowed up, completely. Gone.

"Brooke, what's been going on?"

"I'm not Brooke." My skin prickles. "God, we don't even look anything alike!"

"No, Brooke. You *are* Brooke." He frowns.

"I'm Kira—and this is a really sick joke to play."

Uncle Glenn's eyes widen. "I don't know who Kira is."

"Just stop calling me by my sister's name! My sister who died!"

"Shhhh, please." Uncle Glenn sounds worried and looks up at the ceiling. Then he frowns again. "You didn't have a sister, Brooke. You're an only child."

"No." I shake my head. "No, I'm *Kira*. My sister, Brooke, my *twin*, she died. She was murdered by Mr. Norman, right before he killed our parents."

Uncle Glenn swallows hard. His Adam's apple bobs. "I think I need to phone someone, Brooke. You've been missing for four weeks. We've all been worried. I need to let the team at De Hewitt know—"

"No! I'm not going back there," I cry. "I can't. They'll rebrand me and—"

"Rebrand?" He blinks. The tea-towel starts to slip from his shoulder, but he catches it, holds it awkwardly in his hands that suddenly seem very large.

Upstairs, something starts wailing. High-pitched and angry, and I don't like it. It shouldn't be there.

"Brooke, dear—"

"I'm not Brooke! I'm Kira!"

"Wait, Kira's your middle name, right?" Uncle Glenn frowns, then touches his forehead. "Brooke Kira Taylor."

"What?" Then I shake my head. He's trying to distract me. Is this a test? Another game? A challenge? And that wailing upstairs? That's a test, too. I've got to do something… No, this is distracting me. They're all in on this. "I know my sister," I hiss. "She existed. And she's dead. Mr. Norman killed her. I found her body."

"You found another girl's body, Brooke—uh, Kira." He runs his hands through his hair. "What was her name? Fiona something?"

"Fiona?" I take a step back. Something inside my chest twists.

Uncle Glenn nods. "Barry Norman had been abusing children at your school. Fiona and there was a boy, too. Had a bird name."

A bird name? "Raven."

"Yes. It was, uh, a terrible business. But Brooke—uh, Kira, please, listen. *You* stopped that monster."

"But Brooke died."

"*Fiona* did. Norman murdered her. But because of you, Raven went through no more abuse. He lived. *You* lived."

He's right, Chaos whispers.

Right?

Your sister is you, Kira. She is Brooke. You are Brooke. But you split into two in your mind, a way to cope with it all.

"There was only *one* murder of a child," Uncle Glenn says, and he seems to have trouble saying it, like the words get stuck in his throat and are just sitting there, bobbing about. He looks toward the doorway, to where the hall is. And the stairs.

"Only one…" I shake my head. My uncle is smiling. "It's not a good thing. One murder isn't a good thing!"

"I'm not saying it is. But that man's not a threat anymore. He's locked up."

"Locked up?" I shake my head. "No, he's out there."

He's not, Chaos says.

"They caught him," Uncle Glenn says.

But we were in his car!

That didn't happen. We, uh, hitchhiked. The man just looked a bit like him.

"No!" I shout. "It was him! You told me it was him!"

Uncle Glenn takes a step back. "I need to phone your care coordinator," he says. "I have to." He wanders to the side of the room, to where his phone is plugged in, charging. The wailing upstairs is still alive. The baby monitor is flashing—I suddenly notice the light, red and winking, on the mantelpiece. It's watching me.

And there's a baby.

My eyes widen.

It's my baby. I was in labor in the hospital... Raven's baby.

No, that was the story you told yourself. She's not Raven's.

I freeze.

No. I... This is all ridiculous. I can't have had a baby.

Uncle Glenn sends alarmed looks at me as he unplugs the phone and dials a number. I tune out his words, concentrate on Chaos.

"Why did you go along with this?" I whisper to her, aware of how my uncle's still watching me, even when on the phone. "Why did you pretend that was Mr. Norman in that car? You told me you rescued me from him."

You're unwell, Kira. You really are. You need help, you need to get better.

"I'm fine!"

You're not. And we shouldn't have left The Facility. I'm sorry. I was being selfish. I didn't want to be in that place, too. But the longer we were out there, the more I realized you shouldn't have been. I'm sorry, Kira. But you need to get better.

"I am better, I'm fine!" I yell.

Uncle Glenn jumps. He's talking fast now. His words are like insects.

You will get better, Chaos whispers. *You know the truth now, everything your uncle told you. You can start to accept that. And then you will heal. I promise. Things aren't always going to be like this.*

I dig my fingernails into my thighs. The thin material of the leggings I'm wearing—leggings I don't even recognize— snags on my nails, makes a splintering sound.

"Thank you," Uncle Glenn says, ending his call. "It's all right…Kira. You're back with me now. It will be all right."

I wait for Chaos to say something.

She doesn't.

"We need to pack you a bag," Uncle Glenn is saying. "We're going to drive straight there, and we're going to meet Matt at the hospital. I'll get Annabel ready and—"

"The hospital?" I interrupt.

"The De Hewitt Hospital," he says.

My head spins. "I don't want to go back there. I don't want that branding put back!"

"You won't have a branding put back," he says. "I promise." He holds his hand out. "Come on."

I stare at his hand.

It's okay, Chaos says. *We'll have more fun when you're better.*

"We can have fun now," I whisper, and a tear slides down my face.

We can't, Kira. You have to get better first.

WEDNESDAY, JUNE 11TH, 2014
THREE MONTHS AFTER MISS
TAYLOR'S SECOND ADMISSION
TO THE DE HEWITT HOSPITAL

Getting Better

"THESE WERE ALL SYMPTOMS OF PSYCHOSIS you were experiencing," Dr. Matt Harper says. "Thinking people are trying to harm you. Delusions. Hearing voices. And postpartum psychosis is—"

"Voices?" I shake my head. "But I never heard voices."

He looks back at his notes. "You called her Chaos. You spoke of her a lot, when you first came back to us." His face is sympathetic. "I wish you'd been more honest with us before, when you first were with us. We could've helped you so much more if we'd known all of this."

I just stare at the celebrity selfies. My lower jaw aches, and I'm not sure why. "Am I always going to be like this?"

"Are you *still* getting all those symptoms?" he asks. "You haven't talked about Chaos for a long time."

"I haven't heard her," I say. I grip my hands together. My skin still itches to be written upon, but I haven't done that in nearly a month now. I've never seen my body look so clean, so normal. "Chaos disappeared the second week back here." It was the afternoon after Raven visited me. He seemed so out of place here, but he smiled at me.

"Then you're getting better, Kira."

It feels like a small victory that they've let me keep my identity. I feel better, as Kira. Even if things aren't quite right yet. "But it's the medication. That's just stopping her."

"Kira, you have to understand that what you've been through, what you're going through, is a lot. You endured some very traumatic experiences, being sexually assaulted along with other children, and then discovering the body of your friend. You and Fiona were close. That's what you told me. You became friends because you both understood each other. Your shared experiences allowed a great bond to develop between the two of you. And we already know that when someone close dies, there is a chance it can trigger a psychotic episode or illness in a loved one.

"You endured Fiona's death. *And* the deaths of your parents. As well as the pregnancy, and of course the trauma leading up to all of this, with Mr. Norman."

Norman. Not *Mr.* Norman. I want to correct him. That man doesn't the honor of being called *Mr.* But I don't, I just stare numbly at my hands.

"And the pregnancy. I mean, postpartum psychosis can occur without any of the other traumas you experienced. And the alcohol you drank regularly while on your voyage can't have helped the psychosis either."

The *voyage.* Part of me wants to snort. That's what they all call it. Like I'm some eighteenth-century heroine on a ship.

"Nor the unfortunate fact that you managed to get caught up in Emilia Johnson's disappearance." He shakes his head. "It is a lot for anyone to cope with, and given all this, I have to say, Kira, you're coping remarkably well. And we will get you better. It will take time, but we will do it, Kira. And you have already made great progress, don't forget that."

I try to smile, but I don't feel like smiling. My head feels clearer now. Clearer than it has done in a long time.

I remember things now. Like discovering the body. And it was Fiona. Not my sister.

I don't have a sister.

I'm alone. Except for Annabel.

My daughter. That's what everyone says. But although I remember things, I can't really remember her. She was the second survivor that my old neighbor spoke of. Me and Annabel.

Uncle Glenn visits me here, at the De Hewitt Hospital, every single day now, apart from Wednesdays, because that's when he's sleeping as he works the Tuesday nightshift. Sometimes, he brings Annabel, other times she stays with the babysitter. I prefer the days when she isn't there. Because I don't connect to her. I don't really connect to anyone.

But Uncle Glenn looks after her. So I guess she can be his child now. Because she can't be mine. I can't be her mother. I can't even look at her. Even though none of this is her fault. But her features bring me too much pain.

They caught him though—Norman. I don't have to worry about him showing up, they say. Uncle Glenn tells me this every day I see him. And every time I see Uncle Glenn, he also says he's sorry that he didn't visit *before*. He was still getting used to the new way of things. And I suppose a screaming baby was enough, let alone a psycho niece.

Psycho. I'm not supposed to use that word. No one likes it when I say that word.

"I'll see you tomorrow, Kira," Matt says, and again, I'm glad they do still call me by my middle name. The doctors all agreed that taking on a new name and identity was a coping mechanism. Apparently, it's not uncommon.

Uncle Glenn still slips up from time to time and calls me Brooke. But he's trying.

Everyone's trying.

Most of all, me.

Note from the Author

GIRL, VANISHING IS A STORY ABOUT MENTAL illness and trauma, abuse and healing, and in writing this story I thought a lot about the language I would use. There is so much power held within words, and a lot of the time, the power that words hold can be—and is—misused. Kira uses ableist language to describe herself, her illness, and her world: the words *stupid, crazy*, and *insane*, for example, are ableist and have roots in eugenics, which have negative connotations when it comes to how disability is viewed. The fact that Kira and the other patients at The De Hewitt Hospital use words such as these for themselves but that they object strongly when a nurse uses them, depicts their reclamation of this ableist language, as they try to get their power back. Yet we cannot ignore the roots of this language.

I thought long and hard about the inclusion of such language in this book, and I was advised by sensitivity readers qualified to read for disability representation, but ultimately, I decided to keep these words. Words do have power, and while I could have changed *stupid* for *worthless* and *crazy* for *ridiculous*, this would have changed the tone too much for me and we would've lost this power within the language. After all, *Girl, Vanishing* is about language and the words we use.

In my early twenties, I experienced hallucinations and obsessive behavior as a result of brain inflammation. I was in an out of hospital, routinely reviewed by psychiatrists, and I remember just how much power words had. I hated the word *psychosis* because I'd only come across this word before when stigma had been attached to it. When the doctor mentioned this word during an appointment, I wanted to rip the word up and throw it away. I felt like being labeled *psychotic* took my power away and meant no one would believe me. When I was prescribed antipsychotics, I was adamant I didn't need them—the prescription meant I was being brushed off as *mad* and I did not take that medication because those words were being used to silence me and I desperately wanted my voice to be heard.

Yet I was, at varying points, aware of how warped my reality was. I was obsessive, convinced birds were flying around me, certain that insects were following me, sometimes even spending hours of the day searching my room for these birds and insects, yet part of me could also see beyond the psychosis at times. I felt like I was living inside a distorted mirror. I knew that things weren't quite right—but I also felt powerless not to believe in my delusions.

There are certain words Kira falls back on constantly in this story: *stupid, alone, insane,* and *idiot* were taken straight from the diaries I kept during this time, as were *mirror mirror on the wall* and *help help help*, alongside a few others. This language was authentic to my own experience of hallucinations and disrupted reality, and while I did not have postpartum psychosis, nor had I experienced the trauma Kira has, it was important to me for her words to reflect my experiences.

Writing this story was incredibly healing for me, and Kira finds writing therapeutic too, embodying these words on her skin. And, by the end of *Girl, Vanishing*, we see Kira is beginning to acknowledge her own internalized ableism and starting to change the language she uses, such as when she comments that 'psycho' is not a word she should be using.

RESOURCES

I UNDERSTAND THAT THERE IS A LOT OF content in this book that could be triggering, so if you need support, please reach out to a trusted person, organization, charity, or medical professional. Included below are details for organizations and charities that may be able to help. These details are correct as of the time of publication and are mainly UK-centric. If you are outside of the UK, please seek out equivalent support in your community.

Mental Health Support

- Mind.org.uk, call 0300 123 3393 or email info@mind.org.uk

- Samaritans, call free on 116 123

- Rethink, call on 0300 5000 927

Rape and Sexual Abuse Support

- 24/7 Rape and Sexual Abuse Support line, for individuals 16+ years, call free on 0808 500 2222

- SARSAS, call on 0808 801 0456

- The Survivors Trust, call on 0808 801 0818

- Galop (for LGBT+ Survivors), call 0800 999 5428

Child Abuse Support

- Childline (for children) call 0800 1111

- NSPCC (for adults), call 0808 800 5000 or email help@NSPCC.org.uk

ACKNOWLEDGMENTS

Girl, Vanishing is a story I've wanted to tell for a long time, and I am so grateful to everyone who's helped me shape this book. Firstly, I need to thank the early cheerleaders of Kira's story for keeping me motivated: Lisa Amowitz, Emily Colin, Heidi Ayarbe, and Sarah Anderson.

To my wonderful critique partners, beta readers, and sensitivity readers: Teri Terry, Sara Grant, Lindsay Smith Sellers, Josie Jaffrey, Annette Caseley, and Lara Ameen—thank you so much for your feedback and guidance.

Next, I must thank my amazing editor, Emily Colin. You've really made this book shine! And thanks also goes to Sarah Anderson for the cover art and interior design.

I couldn't have written this book without the support of my family. To Mum, Dad, Sam, Gill, and my in-laws, thank you. But the biggest thank-you goes to my husband Michael, without whom I wouldn't have had the courage to publish this story. Thank you for always believing in me.

About the Author

MADELINE DYER lives in the southwest of England, where she hangs out with her Shetland ponies and writes dark and twisty young adult books. She is pursuing a PhD in Creative Writing from the University of Bristol, having obtained an MFA in Creative Writing from Kingston University and a BA honors degree in English from the University of Exeter. Madeline has a strong love for anything dystopian or ghostly, and she can frequently be found exploring wild places. At least one notebook is known to follow her wherever she goes.

Girl, Vanishing is her eighteenth book.

She also writes as Elin Annalise.

www.ingramcontent.com/pod-product-compliance
Lightning Source LLC
Chambersburg PA
CBHW051002210726
48287CB00004B/1335

* 9 7 8 1 9 1 2 3 6 9 5 0 8 *